Where The Heart Belongs

Jay .H. Dee

Scripture taken from the New King James Version®. Copyright © 1982 by Thomas Nelson, Inc. Used by permission. All rights reserved.

Cover Photos from the Createspace collection.
Cover design from a template in the Createspace cover creator collection.

Where The Heart Belongs

www.jayhdee.weebly.com

ISBN 978-0-9942436-4-5

Dedicated to my nephews.
May you grow to be
awesome men of God,
history makers for Him!
You boys are stars.

Acknowledgements

Thanks to my family and friends who are my faithful readers, constructive critics and greatest supporters. Most of all thanks to You, Lord. I can't write a sentence unless you drop in Your inspiration. You're my number one partner in all I do. All credit is totally Yours. Thank You for all that You are and all that You've done. Be glorified!

Prologue

Wyoming:

"You'll never amount to anything! You're always under my feet, always getting in the way. You should have died with him!" Rylan Jackson waved his arm wildly in an angry gesture.

Laina cringed at the odor on her uncle's breath as he hurled his words at her like daggers. His hand drew back, and being cornered in the kitchen, she had nowhere to escape the coming blow. She braced herself.

His open hand connected with her face and the world momentarily tilted on its axis. Her back slammed into the pantry door and her knees buckled. She slid to the floor, landing with a jarring thud. Spots danced before her eyes and she blinked to clear her vision.

It returned in time to see him turn away and stagger toward the living room.

Laina's fingers gingerly touched her smarting right cheek.

"I wish I had." The broken whisper tore from her throat and silent tears spilled over her lashes. She had learnt early on that crying aloud only made him angrier.

Laina picked herself up off the floor and placed a steadying hand on the marble countertop. Her eyes darted toward the living room where the television suddenly blared. Football. It was Friday night. Give him twenty minutes and he would be passed out drunk on the couch. Good!

She was dying here, maybe not physically, but in every other way. Only two years ago in Chicago, she had been happily talking with her dad in the car on the way home from school. Yet in one moment of time, it had all changed. That life seemed so far away now. A distant memory.

Her father's words from their last conversation when she was thirteen, played over in her mind unbidden. *"You have choices. You don't have to be anyone's doormat. Stand up, step out and lose your fear. God is bigger than any problem you will ever face..."*

He had been referring to the local bully giving her a hard time. Laina shook off the memory and scuffed to the staircase. Her leaden feet took the stairs slowly.

"You have choices... You have choices..."

Connor Jackson's words echoed in her mind in a steady cadence that matched her footsteps. She was tired of living her life as her uncle's doormat. She was tired of being a victim.

"You have choices..."

Bitter tears stung the back of her eyes. "What choices do I have?"

"You have choices... Stand up, step out and lose your fear..."

Laina paused on the top step as a drop of clarity illuminated her thinking. Yes, that was what held her back. Fear. Fear of the unknown, fear she would not be able to fend for herself, and worst of all, fear that if she didn't do something soon, she would be forever trapped in this nightmare.

"I *am* scared." She swiped angrily at the trails of moisture on her cheeks. "So I guess I'll just have to do it afraid."

Resolve hardened her classic features and she strode purposefully to her room down the hall. She plucked her backpack from the floor by the door and stuffed her most valuable things inside. Her mother's locket, her father's Bible, and the family photo album.

Laina was ready to pack her clothes and blankets too when she realized the ramifications of running away. Rylan would have the authorities find her and then there would be more trouble than she could imagine.

She stopped and let her gaze wander her room. No, she would leave it reasonably intact. She might even return now and then if she had a need, for example to have him sign school documents.

Rylan was a workaholic and generally paid her comings and goings little mind. She was only a hindrance to his comfortable, carefree life. No, she would not run away entirely. He was her guardian and no questions would be asked while she 'officially' lived under his roof.

But when Rylan was home, she would make sure she was somewhere else. She knew just the place too. Laina closed the door and slid the bolt into place. She huddled in bed rubbing her sore face and waited for daylight to enact her plan.

~

Laina stared up at the cubby house nestled securely in the sturdy arms of a massive oak. She did not know who had built the one window, one door structure, only that it had been there since she arrived two years ago and probably for several years before that.

The large oak tree was the perfect haven for the little house and she had no fear that storms or fierce weather would bring it down. It stood in a small clearing beside a river, Icy Creek to be exact, and was surrounded on all sides by towering native trees. A ten minute walk south through the woods led directly to town. To the north was mountain range after mountain range covered in majestic forests, through which ran the occasional hunting track. Otherwise the wilderness was unspoiled.

Laina spent her weekend doing a few repairs to the little house, such as adding a bolt to the door and plugging a few gaps in the shingled roof. The glass in the window was still intact, so she did not worry that she would have any uninvited forest dwellers coming to call. The addition of a rope ladder gave her better access to her new home.

Bit by bit she filled the tree house with her things. A rug for the floor, pictures for the walls, a wooden chest for her clothes, an inflatable bed, and blankets to keep her warm.

In the coming week she applied for a job at Gracie's Diner and was hired. She hoped that in time she would be totally independent of her uncle. All the same, she was off to a good start.

1

One year later:

Zachariah Delaney dropped his bag at his feet and stared numbly at his new room. It was void of furniture, which his mother promised would be arriving any minute now. The small country house was an empty shell, much like he felt. After the death of his father a year ago, his life had become as desolate and bleak as the arid Sahara.

"This is a great house, Zach!" His mother came from her own room across the hall and stood in his doorway. "Have you checked out the backyard?"

"No," he replied blandly, wishing they could have stayed in New York.

"It backs onto the woods. It looks like a great place to go exploring."

"And get eaten by a bear no doubt." Zach's pessimism was a steady downpour of gloom upon Caroline's sunshiny day.

"I know you wanted to stay in New York, Zach, but this move is for the best. You'll see. A fresh start will do us both good."

"What's wrong with me living with Mike?" Zach turned to face her, resentment surfacing quickly.

"Your brother is twenty-two years old and is working full-time to pay his own way. He can't be looking out for you as well. Besides, it's not his job to be a parent. So for now you'll just have to survive living with your bossy mother." A teasing light entered Caroline's eyes. She impulsively kissed his cheek and ruffled his hair and then breezed from the room in a disgustingly happy mood.

Zach wiped his cheek with a sleeve in disdain. "Come off it, Mom! I'm not five anymore. Do you have to keep doing that?"

"You may be sixteen, son, but you'll always be my baby," she hollered from the kitchen.

Zach could picture her face... cheeky gleaming eyes and a teasing grin. He wasn't too far off the mark. Caroline flung open windows and doors in joyful abandon to air the cottage.

~

Golden rays of sunlight poured through the tree

house window onto Laina's sleeping face. Her battery alarm clock loudly announced the arrival of another day. She groaned and shut it off. She opened her eyes a crack and was blinded by the sun's morning glory.

"Good morning Lord." A peaceful smile stole over her face. She stretched luxuriously and ventured forth from beneath her quilt. She sleepily pulled on a pair of faded cut off jeans and a blue T-shirt. It was a warm morning.

There was only one more day left of school before summer break. That meant test results would be in. Laina could not afford to miss school, and indeed rarely ever did. She was determined to prove her uncle wrong. She *would* amount to something.

Once dressed, Laina read her Bible and chatted with God. The past year of solitude and total reliance upon Him had knitted a strong bond and forged a fire-tried faith. She could honestly say she was no longer living on the faith of her father.

After feeding her spirit she fed her body. Her small stash of canned and packet goods was getting low, but then payday was not far around the corner. She went home less and less nowadays, but thankfully Uncle Rylan seemed not to notice. And if he did, he did not appear to care. Judging by his loss of weight and more withdrawn manner, he had other worries on his mind.

Laina slapped together a peanut butter sandwich for lunch, tossed her books into her pack and climbed down from her tree house. Sunlight filtered through the canopy of leaves rustling gently in the morning breeze. Lush green grass surrounded the area, also gracing the banks of Icy Creek, which rippled steadily not fifteen paces from the tree house. Wild flowers dotted the small grassy clearing, even daring to venture into the forest standing majestically on all sides.

Laina smiled. This was home now. The tree house was her haven of peace and freedom, the night sounds a welcome lullaby and the woods a beautiful home where solace and the presence of God abounded.

After a drink and a wash from the creek, she ambled happily along the forest trail to town and then on to school.

~

Laina glanced down at her test as her Math teacher passed the graded papers out. She smiled. An A+ was boldly printed at the top of the page. She had studied incredibly hard in the evenings by torchlight to get that mark.

Desks lined the classroom, each one occupied by a student either waiting for a graded test from Mrs.

Whittaker traversing the aisles, or already studying the mark they had received. There were many smiles, even the occasional joke over a pass or fail grade.

However, the envious stare Allie turned on Laina from two desks over gave her a nagging feeling in the back of her mind. Clearly Allie had done poorly. Laina felt sorry for her, also a little wary. Allie had changed. She had gone from girl next door to fashion plate.

Laina had never cared what her former friend looked like and still didn't. Allie's self-image was quite low and she sought to boost it by pulling Laina down. Her minor jealousy of a year ago had now grown into a monster that had devoured their friendship.

"Congratulations to those of you who have worked hard this semester. You've earned a well deserved break." Mrs. Whittaker returned empty handed to the front of the class. "I'm happy to inform you that there will be no homework assignments over the summer and-"

The room erupted in a collective jubilant cheer, cutting the teacher off halfway through her announcement. Laina grinned and noted Mrs. Whittaker's kind blue eyes crinkling warmly at the corners. Her sandy colored hair fell to her shoulders in soft waves that bounced as she chuckled.

She waved her hand to quiet the class. "I can see you're all heartbroken by the news. The bell is about to go, so let me just say this: have a fun break and stay safe."

As if on cue, the bell rang, announcing the beginning of summer holidays. Students piled out of classrooms on both sides of the corridor. The atmosphere was loud and celebratory.

Laina moved along with the stream of bodies until she reached her locker. She stowed her books, glad to be giving her eyes a rest for a while. She slung her pack over her shoulder and was about to head for the nearest exit, a door across the hallway that led to a large area of lawn edged by flower beds. She paused when she recognized her name falling from the glossed lips of one of the popular girls Allie now hung out with.

Laina caught several disparaging remarks regarding her faded, worn apparel and her cheeks flamed red. Allie glanced at her wearing a haughty smile. The demeaning way her eyes slid over Laina's clothes was enough to make the sixteen-year-old feel like a fish out of water. She was tempted to fade into the crowd and simply skulk away. Then she strengthened her resolve.

She crossed the hallway and came to a stop directly in front of the three girls. Laina's expression was kind but frank.

"Allie, is there something I've said or done to upset

you?"

Her friends exchanged smug glances while the girl in question had the good grace to look ashamed.

Laina's forthright gaze then encompassed the others. "Does anyone else have something they need to discuss with me?"

Awkwardness came over the group and silence prevailed.

"Alright. I'll assume that everything is okay. I hope you all have a nice break." Laina forced a smile, nodded goodbye and walked away. She noticed as she did that conversation did not follow her, nor did any snide remarks.

Laina prayed for them as she walked the short distance to Gracie's Diner in the center of town. She had no enemies and knew she should not be picky or choosey with whom she shared God's love.

The bell over the diner door jingled as she entered.

"Laina honey, ya showed up just in the nick o' time!" Gracie Seaton called from behind the counter.

The room was abuzz with lively teenage chatter. Tables and booths were quickly becoming packed with the after school crowd who were eager to start off the summer holidays with a celebration soda.

Laina dumped her pack in a corner of the kitchen before donning an apron and then taking up pencil and paper to record orders.

"Where do you want me to start, Gracie?"

"With that booth in the corner, then work your way across. I ain't been able to get away from the kitchen yet."

Laina smiled at Gracie's seemingly flustered mood. Secretly she enjoyed it when her place was packed with the youth of Icy Creek. Gracie was rather ample, with red curly hair. Laina guessed her to be in her late fifties.

"Yes ma'am."

"When there's a lull, there's a piece o' pie waitin' for ya in the kitchen." Gracie passed her employee a smile and mischievous wink. "Ya must be starved after a long day at school."

Laina grinned in answer. She was hungry, and until payday, food would be a little scarce. "Thanks Gracie!"

"Anytime honey."

Laina went straight to work. She didn't get around to that piece of pie until nearly six o'clock. By then she was ravenous and wolfed it down in a matter of minutes, also enjoying a milkshake.

Gracie dropped onto a chair at the small table tucked in a corner of the kitchen. This was where Laina was sitting.

"Phew!" The older woman sighed and looked at her. "That was wild."

Laina smiled around her straw and sucked up the last mouthful. "Sure was."

"You'd think they'd never eaten with the way they basically inhaled all I baked this mornin'!"

"Thanks for saving me a piece of pie." Laina smiled at her friend.

"You earned it honey." Gracie's gaze suddenly became curious. "What ya gonna do with all that time ya got this summer?"

"Work for you and maybe do some fishing." Laina shrugged.

Gracie frowned. "Why d'you work so hard in this crummy diner for an ol' woman when you got a rich uncle? Don't he feed ya or somethin'?" Her shrewd gaze drifted over Laina's worn cut off jeans and faded T-shirt.

Laina knew that although she was always clean, she didn't look like she'd had a new article of clothing in a very long time. She disguised her sudden discomfort with a joking remark.

"Do you want me to slack off for a while and make a little more mess?"

Gracie smiled, although her perceptive eyes still studied her. "I was just curious."

Laina mentally squirmed. If anyone ever found out her situation, the welfare department would step in and turn her world upside down. She did not want to be uprooted again, or worse yet to end up in the system. She only had to make it another two years and then she would be of age to do whatever she wanted.

"There's nothing wrong with a little financial independence or responsibility, Gracie," she commented with twinkling eyes, hoping the astute woman would not see beyond the flippant facade.

Gracie exhaled slowly and rose. "Ya got a point there. Wish all my employees worked as hard as you." She began to bustle around the kitchen. There was a mountain of dishes and a diner full of tables to wipe down.

Laina sighed with relief. Her secret was safe for now. She dropped her empty plate and cup onto one of the trays that Gracie was about to run through the industrial dishwasher, and pitched in with the evening cleanup. Her next shift wasn't until Monday afternoon. She was looking forward to a relaxing weekend.

2

Laina basked in the warm morning sunshine. Her feet dangled idly in the river, tickled gently by the current whispering through her toes. Her second-hand fishing pole, bought at a local garage sale only last summer, was held loosely in her hands. The line was slack and attached to it was a trout float bobbing playfully in the stream. She was in her element.

Her food box was down to two cans and three slices of bread. Although she wasn't thrilled about it, she wasn't stressing either. A decent sized trout or two would keep her going for today, and today was all she had to worry about.

There was a brief tug on the other end of her line and Laina smiled. She waited a few more seconds before there was a more decisive bite. She gave the pole a swift upward lift to hook the fish and tightened the slack. The tip of the fishing rod bent almost double and she came to her feet. She had a fighter on. With a grin for the thrill of the battle, Laina reeled a large trout out of the river and onto the bank. She dealt the death blow with a thick stick and tossed the poor victim into a bucket of water to keep fresh. One more like that and she would have a feast.

She was just baiting her hook again when a twig behind her snapped. She spun around, wide eyes alert and scanning the forest. Her search stopped twenty yards beyond her tree house.

Standing just at the edge of the clearing in trendy shorts and T-shirt, brown hair spiked fashionably with gel, was a teenage boy Laina guessed to be about her age. She had never seen him before.

Both teens stared warily at one another. Laina rarely had visitors and those that did come calling were usually of the four legged variety. What if the location of her secret hideaway got out? She hoped he would think this was merely a fishing spot.

"Hi," she greeted with as casual a wave as she could muster. "I've got to say that you're the first human I've seen all morning."

"It's no wonder out here." His eyes disdained the remote forest around him.

Laina calmly finished baiting her hook and cast it into the stream. "I haven't seen you around before. What's your name?"

The boy ambled across the clearing, first glancing up at the tree house as he passed under it and then peering into the bucket close to where Laina was fishing. "Nice fish. I saw you pull it in."

"Yeah, it's pretty big. It'll make a tasty lunch. So, you still haven't answered my question."

The stranger glanced up and met her gaze. He had dark brown eyes. Quite a different shade to her light blue. His were guarded, full of depth and yet unwilling to tell their story.

"Zach. And yours?" Everything about his expression and stance said he would give only as much as was polite.

"Laina. Where you from?" She sat down on the grassy bank, hoping the boy would either relax a little or decide to move on.

"Icy Creek. My mom just bought a house on the edge of these woods."

Laina let her gaze wander to the stream rippling happily by. "D'you fish?"

Zach frowned in bewilderment. "Not really. Well, not ever."

"Then you'd better sit down and take this pole for a while. There's nothing quite like the honorable battle between fish and man... well, girl in my case." Laina smiled and offered him the rod and at the same time reached out in friendship.

Zach snorted, yet sat and took the pole. He kicked off his shoes and stuck his feet in the water as Laina had done. "What do I do if I get one?"

"Try not to scare it off with that scowl on your face," she advised with wickedly gleaming eyes.

Zach's gaze snapped to meet hers. When he realized he has being teased, a reluctant smile made an appearance.

"You should try that more often." Laina indicated the smile that evidenced a warm personality under his defensive exterior.

"Haven't got a whole lot to smile about." He focused on the float bobbing blithely in the same water that now lapped about his ankles.

"I don't know about that." Laina looked at him thoughtfully.

Zach glanced at her sideways. "What's that supposed to mean?"

"Only that you're sitting in the middle of a beautiful paradise on a gorgeous summer day with a cool river to dip your feet in. There's no work to do, except to engage in the timeless art of a bygone era." She smiled contentedly, thoroughly enjoying her surroundings.

"You talk like an old person." His smile was lopsided. "I've got no idea what you just said, but it sounded good."

Laina laughed. There was something about that hearty, carefree sound that made Zach relax.

"I guess I read too many books. So, why are you

23

down in the dumps?"

The effect of her kind eyes combined with her open manner was enough to cause Zach to take his guard down.

"I want to go home."

"What city were you originally from?"

"How'd you know I'm a city kid?" He looked at her sideways in surprise.

Laina smiled. "It takes one to spot one."

"You lived in the city?"

"Yeah." She did not talk much about that part of her life anymore. Most people just weren't interested. "My dad and I lived in Chicago till I was thirteen. Where are you from?"

"New York. It sure beats living in a hole like Icy Creek." Zach's bitterness over the move was almost tangible.

"Yeah, you gotta miss the smell of pollution, the congested traffic and sirens going off at all hours of the day and night," Laina replied sarcastically.

Zach stared at her and finally broke into an amused smile. A sudden tug on the end of his line brought on a measure of excited panic. "I think I've got one."

"Well, reel it in, and whatever you do don't let it get away!"

Zach worked hard and with the help of his coach, he landed a decent sized trout. For the first time, he smiled a full blown grin. "Just wait till I tell Mom. She'll never believe me."

"Why don't you take it home for her?" Laina removed the hook from its mouth and killed it the same way she had done the other.

"She'd probably freak out with its head still attached and those beady eyes staring at her." He studied the hapless creature in fascination.

Laina chuckled. "Then I guess you're just going to have to stay for lunch. We'll cook them over the campfire."

Zach glanced curiously about at the clearing. "What campfire?"

"The one we're going to build."

He held her gaze and they both grinned. It was the beginning of a fun day and a good friendship.

~

"Hey stranger," Laina greeted Zach Monday afternoon two days later.

He was sitting at a table in Gracie's Diner. She stood by his table with pencil and paper in one hand and the other on her hip. Her friendly smile seemed to put Zach instantly at ease. Memories of pulling several fish from the river on Saturday and frying them over a campfire, making him laugh at himself the whole time, brought forth a huge welcoming smile.

He smiled in return. "How's it goin' Laina? I didn't know you worked here."

"Yeah, I've worked for Gracie for a year now. What did you get up to on Sunday?"

Zach shrugged nonchalantly. "Not much a guy can do around here."

Laina's gaze narrowed over his sullen attitude. "Yeah, I know what you mean. What with all those mountains and trees everywhere it's kind of hard to come up with something adventurous to do."

Zach's unimpressed stare met her amused one. "Can I get a soda and fries," he changed the subject. "And hold the sarcasm."

Laina's eyes twinkled mischievously and a smile played at the corners of her mouth. "Sure. What flavor?"

"Coke." Zach stared at the salt and pepper shakers in the center of the table and his fingers idly fiddled with a sugar sachet.

Laina made a note of his order. "Is that with or without ketchup?"

"With."

"And would you like a free smile with that?"

Zach's head snapped up and he stared at her in confusion. "What?"

"Well, smiles around here are for free, but there is

a catch. They're contagious. If we give you one you'll walk out of here with a silly smile of your own which may start a chain reaction in town."

"You're crazy, you know that." Zach stared at her as though she had lost her mind.

Laina held her hands up in surrender. "Alright, but don't say I didn't warn you. When you walk out of here with a ridiculous grin on your face don't blame me."

Zach frowned in annoyance. "I don't want the free smile."

"Yeah, imagine passing that onto the town. We certainly can't have people feeling happy!" She turned and walked away.

Laina stepped into the kitchen and tore the order from her note pad. She taped it with the others in a long line along the edge of the counter where Gracie was cooking up a storm. She then moved back to the serving area and reached for the glass refrigerator door.

Laina paused with her hand on the handle. Zach was staring miserably out the diner window, watching pedestrians wander past. He looked utterly bored. She observed the lack of haste the citizens on the sidewalk displayed, and mentally compared the quiet country life here to the city she had grown up in. She too had undergone a huge adjustment to small town ways and found herself sympathizing.

Laina sighed and took a can of cola from the fridge and brought it to the counter. She was reaching for a glass when the bell over the door jingled and a tall, strapping teenager walked in. His piercing green eyes scanned the occupants in the room, curiously assessing the new boy before coming to rest on two of his friends in the corner booth at the other end of the diner.

He strode past Zach, who was paying him little heed as he fiddled with the napkin holder in sheer boredom, and sat with his friends. The young man carried a chip on his shoulder the size of Texas.

"Oh anyone but him," Candice bemoaned from beside Laina.

"Anyone but who?"

Her fellow waitress was staring anxiously toward the booth occupying the corner of the diner. "Logan Mathews, who else?" The younger girl glanced at her hopefully. "Will you take his order?" Her eyes were pleading.

Laina sighed. She understood how Candice felt and a year ago she too would have run a mile from the troubled teen. But not now. She was nobody's victim and Logan Mathews was very much in need of Christ's love.

"Okay. Will you take this soda to Zach?" She indicated the teenager staring moodily out the diner window.

Candice nodded with relief and they traded tasks. She served Zach while Laina drew a deep breath, took up pencil and note pad and strode across the room.

Logan and his two friends looked up as she approached. Nick offered a friendly smile, while Wil's eyes went straight back to the map spread on the table before them. Logan's gaze was unreadable.

"How's it going guys?"

"Fine thanks, Laina. Done any fishing lately?" Nick inquired amicably.

"Yeah, on Saturday." She pointed to the newcomer. "I caught three trout and Zach over there caught one. You?"

"Fished down at the bend near the old mill yesterday and caught nothing. We're looking at a map of the area hoping to find a better spot that's not been fished out. Hey, is he new in town?" Nick indicated Zach with a nod of his head.

"Yeah. He's from New York. You'll like him."

"Is he staying long?" Logan's tone said he hoped not.

"A good question. You'll have to ask him," Laina replied with a kind smile, to which he did not respond. "What can I get you guys?"

Nick put in an order and Wil mumbled his, glancing up shyly at Laina to do so.

"And you?" She waited patiently for Logan to state what he wanted.

"I wish all those city folks'd just stay away from Icy Creek and leave us in peace. They're crowding the joint with all those new estates," he growled with a surly scowl toward Zach. "Go back to where you belong, city boy!"

Laina rolled her eyes over the stereotypical opinion. She did not mince matters. "Cut the garbage, Logan, and tell me what you want."

Logan's scowl turned on her and she stared right back. He acquiesced and mumbled an order. Laina nodded decisively and took it down.

"Good. I'll be back with your food shortly." She walked away seemingly unruffled.

Logan's disgruntled gaze bored into Zach's angry stare. As Laina passed by, Zach caught her wrist. She looked down at him in surprise.

"Is that guy bothering you?" His angry eyes shifted from her face to Logan's unrelenting glare.

Laina was stunned that Zach was ready to leap to her defense. She studied him and her gaze softened. "Thanks for looking out for me Zach, and no, he's not bothering me. There's more to Logan than you think."

Zach snorted in disagreement. "He's a moron, Laina."

"Cut him some slack?"

As he stared into the kind eyes of his new friend he relented, albeit grudgingly.

3

"How is the design progressing?" the shady for-eigner asked over the telephone.

"It's nearly finished," the nervous technician re-plied.

"When do I get the blueprints?"

The technician mentally squirmed. His palms were moist and beads of sweat were forming along his hairline. His anxious gaze flitted around his home. It was a beautiful place on a prime piece of real-estate in Icy Creek. However, it was crammed with com-puter parts and miscellaneous junk. The whole place was in a state of neglect, giving evidence to the fact its owner was not only a computer nerd, but also a workaholic.

"Soon. We're just ironing out some kinks."

"Good. The money will be in place by the time you contact me next," the foreigner concluded the con-versation. "I am looking forward to doing business with you."

The computer whizz disconnected the line and

sank onto his couch. He felt something crumple beneath his weight. He reached under his backside and removed several empty cardboard takeaway packages from the cushions and tossed them haphazardly on the floor. He then rested his head against the back of the sofa and let out a long, weary sigh. He would be glad when this thing was over and he could stretch out on a luxuriously sunny beach in the pacific.

~

A clattering sound on the side of the clapboard cottage drew Zach's nose out of the comic magazine he was perusing. He waited, still stretched out comfortably on his bed, for a full minute until it came again. It sounded like small stones hitting the side of the house. He frowned in puzzlement and set the magazine aside. He swung his legs to the floor and crossed the small room to his window. He lifted the glass and leaned out.

"Who's there?" he growled into the darkness beyond.

"It's me," a decidedly feminine voice called softly from the back fence.

"Laina?" She had to be out of her mind to be wandering through the woods in the dark. The very idea terrified him.

"No, it's the boogie man!" she replied with some impatience. "Come for a walk."

"Why?"

"I want to show you something."

Zach was dubious. "No. We'll probably get eaten by a bear or something."

Soft laughter drifted on the breeze. He couldn't help but feel a little foolish.

"Why can't you come to the front door like a normal person?" he snapped to cover his embarrassment.

"And have your mother worry that I'm leading you astray? I don't think so!"

"Leading me astray? What century are you from?"

"Zach, are you coming or not?"

He could just make out her silhouette in the darkness. He teetered in indecision. Finally his curiosity got the better of him and he climbed out his window. He strode to the back fence where Laina was waiting outside the gate.

The darkness pressed in on all sides and the eerie outline of the forest looming behind them caused a chill to run down his spine. He would take the darkened streets of New York over those creepy woods any day.

"What's up?"

"I want to give you a glimpse into a soul," Laina explained cryptically as she turned and started walking around the Delaney's block and onto the road leading past Zach's house.

"Where are we going?" He could feel control of his situation slipping through his fingers. Still he kept pace beside her.

"For a guy that's dying for adventure, you sure are a killjoy."

"Yeah? I guess I just don't fancy being mugged or mauled."

Laina laughed outright, an uninhibited mirthful sound. It wheedled a smile from the scared stiff teenager striding beside her.

They passed several more houses, heading further into the heart of town. Street lamps now illuminated their way, stealing some of his trepidation.

"Zach, the only person that would mug you is... Well, I don't know anyone in Icy Creek that would mug you. And as for being mauled, the closest you'll ever come to that here is Mrs. Nichols's dog. It's toothless and it tends to kiss passersby to death."

"Very funny. Now where are we going?"

"You'll see," is all she would say as she led him down a side street into a dingy unkempt part of town.

In the soft glow of street lamps the houses lining

each side of the road appeared from the darkness
like ghostly apparitions, mere shadows of their former glory. They were rundown and neglected, empty
shells with nothing left but memories of better days
gone by. The eerie silence gave Zach the creeps.

Halfway down the street he noticed light in one
window. Its comforting warm glow spilled onto a tidy
rose garden in the front yard. Laina stopped by the
picket fence surrounding the well manicured lawn.

The house itself looked much like the others, di-
lapidated, shabby. But that was only at a first glance.
Upon further scrutiny, Zach realized with a strange
sense of sadness the love and care that had gone
into the garden. Whoever lived here obviously could
not afford repairs on the house, however there was
a simple dignity reflected in the maintenance of the
grounds.

"Who lives here?" All trace of annoyance and bitterness had gone from his voice.

Laina regarded him with gentle eyes. "Come and
see."

Zach followed her inside the gate that hung pre-
cariously on one rusty hinge to the window from
which light spilled. They stood and observed silently
the scene within. As it unfolded, Zach felt shock steal
over him.

A woman, dressed in faded plain clothes and appearing to be in her mid fifties, was sitting in a tattered recliner. She looked positively exhausted. He watched as her eyelids grew heavier and heavier until they finally closed in sleep.

A moment later a familiar young man entered the living room, leading a small girl by the hand. Logan Mathews gently took the girl to the sofa where she automatically sat, avoiding all eye contact. Her movements were stilted and her mannerisms were unusual. She did not seem to be interested in playing with the Lego on the floor. Instead she fiddled with a feather, twirling it in her fingers and staring at it with great fascination.

After seeing that the girl was comfortable, Logan took a thin rug from the back of the sofa and draped it over the sleeping woman's lap. He then sank onto the sofa next to the girl to watch TV.

"The little girl's name is Tia. She's Logan's sister and she's eight years old. She's autistic," Laina explained softly.

Zach's heart twisted with compassion and a good deal of shame.

"The lady asleep in the chair is their mother. A land developer wants them to sell, and even though everyone else in the street has, they won't. This place is all they've got and they'll never be paid what it's worth to them. Logan's mom works full time in a factory in Walkerville from eight in the morning to six at night, six days a week just trying to keep food on the table and the bills paid so they can keep this place. She's done that ever since her husband left her two years ago. Before he left, he used to yell and abuse her. Logan would stick up for her and get beaten for the trouble."

Zach's gaze left the unsettling scene and anger began to bubble inside him. Something about those people hit too close to home, but he couldn't place his finger on what it was. "Why are you telling me all of this?"

Laina held his gaze and seemed to see beyond his anger. The guilt in his eyes must be obvious.

"If you're trying to tell me to stop feeling sorry for myself you can just-"

"Slow down there Zach." Laina held up a hand to stem the angry tide of words. "I wanted you to understand Logan, to see beyond his biting tongue and antisocial behavior to the worried, hurting boy inside."

Zach turned on his heel and abruptly strode from the yard. Laina followed him. He hit the street and she had to jog to catch up. Once in step beside him, she had to lengthen her stride to match his hasty pace. Suddenly he stopped and spun to face her.

"Who do you think you are? You're so righteous

that you have to set everyone else straight, is that it?"

"Of course not! If you want to fit in then you need to understand the people here."

"Who said anything about fitting in?"

"Fine, if you're so bent on making enemies then go for it," she declared and spun away, hands raised in exasperation. She stalked off down the street the way they had come.

Zach rolled his eyes and went after her. "What makes you think I'm bent on making enemies?" he argued when he finally caught up with her.

"Oh nothing really, just the fact you look down your nose at everyone and everything in this town."

Zach supposed she might think him a bigger trial than Logan. "Okay, you've got a point there."

"You bet I've got a point!"

"Well you don't have to rub it in." Zach's temper cooled at the thought of losing the only friend he had in this town. Besides, if he admitted it to himself, deep down he was sure she was right.

Laina stopped walking and faced him again. He looked sheepish.

"Zach, there are no enemies, only lost people in need of Jesus' love."

His past reared its ugly head. "I don't want His kind of love and I don't know anyone in their right mind that would."

Laina studied him in stunned silence. Her expression changed and he knew she had seen past his facade. "What happened that made you stop loving Him, Zach?"

He looked away. His jaw muscles twitched as he fought an inner battle. Finally his hardened gaze locked with her kind one. "He took my dad. What kind of loving God does that?"

Compassionate tears brimmed over long lashes and she glanced away almost absently. Zach was too incensed to care that he had caused her to cry.

"You wouldn't understand!"

"What?" Laina looked at him directly. She appeared to have missed part of what he was saying.

"I don't want anything from you, so just leave me alone alright? My dad's dead and God could have stopped it, but He didn't. I don't want anything to do with Him!" Hurting and also feeling like a first class heel, he stormed off down the street. Guilt nagged at him for leaving her standing there alone in the dark, but anger rode him harder.

4

"I can't believe you let that trout get away," Nick teased Logan as the three teenagers hiked through the woods toward their next fishing spot.

Logan was unable to stop a sheepish smile. "It ain't my fault that snake swam across the creek at me. I hate snakes!"

Only ten minutes ago they had been on a deep bend of Icy Creek that nary a soul had visited in decades, and it had looked like a veritable fish haven. Then a snake had decided on an afternoon swim, spooking all three boys into a frenzied scramble to gather bait and tackle before hightailing it out of there.

Wil suddenly snickered to himself, obviously recalling their hasty retreat, which started the teenagers laughing all over again. Their laughter finally died down and they continued to walk up and down gullies, through dense woods, across clearings and up rises on their way to the next remote fishing spot marked on their map. The trek would be long but hopefully the fish would make it worthwhile.

They trudged through a thick stand of old growth trees and were close to a clearing when suddenly Wil stopped, his head tilted to catch sounds drifting on the summer breeze. Nick halted also and Logan stopped a few paces ahead of them, glancing back impatiently.

"What is it, Wil?" Nick asked curiously. Wil had the best hearing of any person he had ever met.

"Voices." Wil dropped his gear and listened intently.

Logan also sat his rod and pack down. "We're thirty miles from civilization and it's Thursday. Who could possibly be out here?"

Nick did the same. "Sh, I can hear it too."

Logan frowned in puzzlement and strained to hear. It was a gentle whisper on the wind.

"It's coming from that direction." Wil pointed to the rise on their left.

Logan was the first to begin stalking stealthily through the forest up the incline. The ground foliage was not terribly thick, but it was sufficient to keep him hidden as he dropped and belly crawled the last few yards. Nick and Wil followed his lead. With their heads peeking through the scrub, they studied the scene.

Roughly twenty paces along what appeared to be

a plateau, were two men. Although slightly obscured by trees, the three boys were able to get a reasonable view of what was happening.

The first man was helping the second to lift a large square metal case off the ground. Oddly enough, both were wearing suit pants with crisp white shirts. The first gentleman was older and wore glasses over intelligent eyes, and wisps of thinning brown hair were arranged into a comb over. He was small in stature and struggled with the weight of whatever was in that case.

The second man was quite different from the first. He was young, possibly in his thirties, tall and solidly built with tanned skin and wildly curly black hair. His serious eyes were dark, almost ebony, and his patience thinning as quickly as the older man's hair. His spotless white sleeves were rolled up to his elbows, revealing powerful forearms. He was not a man Nick wanted to tangle with. The two were talking as they began walking toward the clearing, unaware they had company.

"So how long do you think it'll be now that we know what's causing the power drainage?" the younger man asked.

"A week I suspect. All we need now is a..." The older gentleman's voice faded into the distance as they exited the woods to the boys' right, about fifty yards away. Their voices could still be heard, however their words were indistinguishable.

Logan, Nick and Wil exchanged baffled glances.

"What was that about?" Nick puzzled in a whisper.

"Beats me, but I'd like to find out." Logan glanced at Wil who wordlessly shrugged, just as mystified as his friends.

Logan grinned, gaining an adventurous gleam in his eyes that Nick did not like. That look usually meant they were headed into trouble.

"What do you say we check it out?" Logan did not wait for a response. He crept back down the slope and moved as silently as a ghost through the trees toward the clearing.

Nick rolled his eyes in exasperation and followed, leaving their gear on the forest floor. Wil did not look happy about the situation. However the idea of being left behind must have been worse, for he slunk after his buddies. They caught up with Logan, who was crouched behind a stout tree trunk peering through shrubbery at the two men loading the case into the back of a fancy black pickup. The men climbed into the vehicle and backed onto a dirt trail. In minutes they were gone.

"Did you get the number plate?" Wil broke their silence.

"Yep." Logan grinned. He repeated the combination of numbers and letters.

Nick smiled in amusement. "I'm guessing Wil's uncle Dan is going to get a few visitors today, right?"

Wil frowned in annoyance and then emitted a defeated sigh. Dan Fisher was one of the local deputies at Icy Creek's Sheriff's Office. He was also very indulgent of his nephew's nosy friends, who had nothing better to do with their time than hang around and pester the man when they weren't off fishing somewhere.

"You bet." Logan retraced their steps to gather their fishing gear. He was a man on a mission.

~

Laina heard the diner door open and glanced up from the cash register where she was getting change for a customer. Zach Delaney entered, looking his usual designer self. Although upon closer inspection, he appeared to be carrying an air of humility.

"Thanks for the fishing tip." Mr. Wryer, a kind retiree who had recently moved to Icy Creek, took his change and smiled at Laina. He donned his cap.

"You're welcome, and don't forget to tell Mrs. Wryer I said hi."

"I won't forget, missy. She asks after you every time she knows I'm stopping by Gracie's." The old man gathered the boxed slices of pie he had purchased for himself and his wife for a morning treat and headed for the door.

Laina watched him go with a warm smile and then turned her undivided attention to Zach. He had seated himself upon a stool at the counter and was looking a little uncomfortable. She approached him on the opposite side.

"What can I get you, Zach?" She kept her tone free of censure.

"Humble pie if you have any?"

Laina smiled and her eyes twinkled with merriment. "Gracie serves plenty of that here. Would you like a double helping?"

"Be merciful," Zach pleaded, his eyes coming alight with humor. "Just the usual serve."

Laina leaned on the counter and suddenly changed the subject. "Are you up for an adventure?"

Zach's expression became wary. "What do you have in mind?"

"A hike to Cottrell Falls." She hadn't been there in about a month.

"When?"

"Tomorrow. We'll leave at eight."

Zach was scandalized. "In the morning?"

It was summer break and Laina suspected by his reaction that he must not rise until noon.

"No, eight at night. That way we'll be able to get ourselves lost. It's more exciting that way."

"Very funny." He dismissed her sarcasm with an unimpressed stare. "Have you ever been there before?"

"Sure, lots of times. Nick took me fishing a couple of years ago and I've been hiking there ever since."

Zach's expression became mischievous. "So what's the deal with you and him?"

Laina's gaze narrowed dangerously and her words were clipped. "Nick and I have a mutual interest in fishing and that's all. Believe it or not, girls and guys can be just friends."

Zach held his hands up in surrender. "Take it easy. It was just a question."

"A very nosy one laden with assumptions."

"There you go again, using big words." Zach's eyes glimmered with a teasing sparkle.

"Don't they have dictionaries in New York?" Laina was still miffed at him over his assumption that she and Nick were girlfriend and boyfriend.

"Obviously not the one you've been reading. Do I need to bring anything?"

"Good shoes for hiking, a sun hat and sunscreen and your lunch. I'll bring the rest."

"Deal. See you at eight."

5

Laina timidly knocked on the Delaney's front door early Saturday morning and stepped back to wait. She had been tempted to linger at the rear fence rather than meet Zach's mother and undergo scrutiny. Then she thought how foolish that would be. In doing so, she might miss a golden opportunity to make another friend.

She waited patiently for whatever reception lay beyond. However, she was not prepared for the beautiful sunny blond in her forties that wrenched open the door with a beaming smile.

"Hello! You must be Laina. Come on in." She opened the door wider and beckoned enthusiastically for the teenage girl on her porch to enter.

Laina dropped the fishing pole in her hand and the pack on her shoulder before entering. She wiped suddenly damp palms on her cut off jeans. The only home she had been in in a year was her uncle's, and then only when the river was frozen and she was forced to use his shower.

"Zach talks about you quite a bit." Mrs. Delaney led her through an open living space to a small country style kitchen.

"Oh," was all Laina could manage as she gazed about at the homey touches this woman had applied to her new house.

Uncle Rylan's mansion was large and well furnished, but its decor was masculine and void of warmth. This cottage had gathered lace, framed by soft curtains, at all of the windows. The cold glossy wooden floors were broken by plush rugs of soft cream, blue and peach. The furniture was in the same gentle hues and appeared to be delightfully comfortable.

Bright sunlight flooded the living room, bouncing off the cream walls and creating a cheerful atmosphere. The kitchen was a pale yellow with a light timber table and chairs, white cupboards and ample bench space. Again, the touches the woman of the house had added gave the room a quaint country feel. A bread box on the counter, a wooden potato bin -both painted with folk art-, a timber cabinet containing crystal and china, a roman numeral Cob & co. clock on the wall and much more.

Laina was feasting her eyes when she realized the room had grown quiet. Her gaze snapped to her host. Mrs. Delaney's eyes gleamed with merriment. When she finally had her guest's attention, she repeated her question.

"Where are you and Zach going today?"

Laina's heart thudded against her rib cage. For some reason, she really wanted to make a good impression on this woman. "Cottrell Falls."

"And you're going to do some fishing?"

Mrs. Delaney leaned against the kitchen counter and smilingly studied Laina, who was standing nervously in the doorway.

"Sure. Some of my biggest catches have been there." She was unable to stop her eyes from straying to the room before her.

"Well, if you and Zach catch anything, bring it on home and I'll cook it up for dinner tonight." The older woman's sparkling brown eyes drew a smile from Laina.

"That sounds wonderful. Is Zach ready to go?"

"Almost. The last time I checked he was gelling his hair."

Laina raised an amused eyebrow. "He's spiking his hair to go fishing in the middle of nowhere?"

Mrs. Delaney smiled mischievously. "I was rather hoping it was because you'll be there."

Laina stared at her host in stunned surprise and then smiled slowly. "Don't even go there, Ma'am."

"It's Caroline."

Laina chuckled. "Okay. But you should probably know that Zach and I are just friends and I plan to keep it that way."

Caroline's teasing eyes glittered with humor. "Pity."

Laina's mouth dropped open in surprise and then she burst into laughter. Zach's mother smiled warmly and the teasing light left her eyes. "I'll go rouse him."

"No need," Zach broke into the conversation and breezed into the room. He dumped a backpack in the doorway leading off the kitchen to the right, presumably to the bathroom and bedrooms. He then plucked a loaf of bread from the bread box on the counter, spread one slice with raspberry preserve and slapped another piece of bread on top. He rifled through a cupboard and came up with a couple of packets of potato crisps.

Caroline frowned. "That's a really nutritious lunch, son."

Zach did not comment. He simply stuffed his goods into his pack, which he then slung over his shoulder. Bye Mom." He started for the door.

Laina watched the way Caroline hid her disappointment at his brisk dismissal and then turned a warm smile on her.

"It was nice to meet you, Laina. I hope I'll see you for supper tonight?"

Laina smiled kindly in return. "I'm looking forward

to it."

The front door opened with Zach's hasty depar-
ture. Laina followed in his wake. She shouldered her
pack and took up her rod, traipsing down the porch
steps to where Zach waited impatiently at the front
gate. She decided to keep her thoughts to herself
regarding his rudeness, choosing to paste on a happy
smile and wave to Caroline Delaney. The woman at
the door waved, a crease between her brows evidence that she was experiencing either anxiety or
hurt feelings.

Laina grew a little cross when Zach did not even
look behind him. Instead he turned toward the
woods. She gave him a testy shove as they walked
side by side.

"What was that for?" Zach frowned at her in annoyance.

"Stop being heartless and give your mother a
wave!" she hissed.

Zach rolled his eyes yet complied with exaggerated
long-suffering. Laina glanced over her shoulder at
the woman now beaming on the front porch and she
smiled to herself. With that happy picture imprinted
in her memory, she led Zach into the woods on an
adventure she knew he would never forget.

~

"Did you do it?" Logan asked eagerly while leaning over the counter at the sheriff's office.

Deputy Dan Fisher sighed wearily and pushed his roller chair from his desk. He ambled around the front bench and leant a forearm upon the counter top. He crossed his right ankle lazily over his left. The three boys had been pestering him about that irritating license plate for three days. Well, at least two of the boys had been pestering him. Wil's expression had been apologetic on each occasion as he hung back near the doorway.

"No Logan, I have not found who the vehicle belongs to. Believe it or not, I've had other more important things to tend to."

"But this is important!"

"And so is the mountain of paperwork piling up on my desk. Now if you don't mind, I have to get back to it." Dan was running rather low on patience.

"Come on, Mr. Fisher, it'll only take you a couple of minutes."

Dan sighed and rolled his eyes. "If I do it, will you leave me alone?"

Logan and Nick exchanged grins.

Logan's smile was downright cheeky. "Yep."

"Fine." He walked to his desk. He sat down and opened the database on his computer to do a search.

Logan and Nick scooted uninvited around the counter and stood looking over his shoulder, while Wil waited uncomfortably by the front entrance. In a matter of minutes Dan had the results.

"Oh." His brows drew together pensively.

"What?" Logan verbally pounced in anticipation.

"It's a government license plate." Dan closed the search.

Nick was curious. "What branch of the government?"

"I really don't care. I've got more important things to do than keep two nosey boys entertained on their summer break." Dan passed Logan and Nick a meaningful stare. He made it quite clear that his tolerance had reached its limit.

The two teenagers exchanged glances and reluctantly left the office. Once outside, Dan saw them heading to Gracie's Diner across the street, involved in intense discussion.

~

"You're kidding me!" Zach grinned and waved off her remark.

Laina's smile changed into a quizzical stare. "I was serious. How else are we going to get across?"

Zach's horrified gaze shifted from his friend to

the ravine dropping away from them. At least thirty feet below the drop off, foaming white water rushed swiftly over large rocks protruding from the river's surface. Before them stretched a thick fallen tree that bridged the fifteen foot gap between each side of the ravine. Its limbs had broken off leaving only a bare log, and from the looks of it, it was slippery.

Zach was outraged. "Are you trying to kill me?"

Laina smiled in amusement, once again seeming to see beyond his explosive response to the fear gripping his heart. "Yes Zach, I'm trying to kill you. I figured pushing you off this log would be the best way. Your body would wash away with the current and no one would suspect foul play."

Zach could not help the laughter that spontaneously burst from deep within his chest. "Very funny."

"I thought it was." She shrugged and stepped onto the log.

Zach's eyes widened fearfully. "You're not actually going to walk across that are you?"

Laina glanced over her shoulder. "Of course I am. I hear the call of a hundred fat happy trout just waiting to leap onto my dinner plate." She carefully put one sneaker in front of the other, her arms stretched out either side of her for balance and her fishing rod in one hand.

"I don't hear any such call. All I can hear are those

rapids down there ready to suck you under when you fall." Zach's alarmed gaze dropped to the water below and then returned to the daring girl who was now almost halfway across.

"You're such a pessimist!"

Zach held his breath and watched her take the last few steps. Finally her feet touched down on solid ground on the other side and Zach exhaled in relief.

"Alright, it's your turn." Laina was flanked by enormous pines stretching proudly toward the sky.

Zach glanced behind him to where the forest in all its height and grandeur stood imposingly over the gorge. It was not too late to turn back. However if he was honest with himself, it was doubtful he would be able to find his way home. He needed Laina as his guide and she was bent on forging ahead to Cottrell Falls. At this point, he did not see any other option except to follow.

He took a deep breath and stepped onto the log. His runners did not have sufficient tread and immediately lost their grip on the smooth surface. He fell sideways, landing in the grass inches from the lip of the gorge. His heart pounded so fiercely he could hear it in his ears.

"I don't think I can do it. My shoes are too slippery."

"Then take them off. You'll do better in bare feet."

Zach stood on trembling legs. What little confidence he had was now shaken. Laina was observing him, and not wanting to feel foolish, he hid his fear behind a mask of determination. He removed his shoes, tied the laces and draped them about his neck. With one uncertain foot in front of the other, he slowly made his way across the log. After what felt like an eternity, he stepped onto the grass on the other side. Laina had been right.

"See, you did it!" She clapped him heartily on the back.

Zach pasted on a smile and squashed his feet back into his shoes. All the while his insides felt like wobbly jelly and his heart hammered against his rib cage. He hoped this was the last surprise she had in store for him today.

6

The sound of water crashing into a pool became increasingly louder as Laina and Zach hiked through the woods. The pitch of the terrain grew steeper. Zach was out of breath but forced himself to push onward, unwilling to allow a girl to show him up. Laina seemed unfazed by the physical exertion, forging ahead like there was no tomorrow.

When at last he thought his lungs would burst, they pushed past thick spruce branches and were greeted with the most wondrous sight Zach thought he had ever seen.

He stared wide eyed at the curtain of water cascading down a large cliff face, tumbling wildly into the pool below. Water from the deep pool was turbulent where the falls broke its surface and yet serene only a matter of yards away. It was roughly ten paces wide and thirty paces long, walled in on three sides by steep rock faces.

The wall down which the water fell and the wall on the left were both a sheer drop. Only a matter of yards from where Laina and Zach had emerged from the woods was the lower entrance to the pool. There a line of rocks formed a sort of dam, causing the overflow to gently topple over into the river below. It formed a miniature waterfall in its own right.

"We're here. So what do you think?"

"Wow!" Zach's eyes thirstily drank in the scene before him and he let go of all pretense.

Laina observed his enraptured expression and smiled. "Yeah I know, lame isn't it? I mean, what I wouldn't give to be in the middle of a traffic jam right now, smelling toxic fumes and listening to people shout obscenities at each other."

Zach chuckled, unable to muster any feelings of irritation when faced with such magnificence.

"Dad used to say that nature is an expression of God's perfect personality." Laina surveyed the splendor around her.

Zach glanced at her and was struck by the beauty radiating from her countenance. Her features had eased into lines of delight and it was like she was surrounded by an aura of peace. In that moment he envied her faith.

"I wish I could believe that God is as good and loving as you say He is, but I just can't," he admitted in a quiet voice.

Laina's gaze swung to his in surprise. She studied

him for a second.

"Zach, bad things happen to those we love and it doesn't mean that God doesn't care. I believe His willingness to walk through those tragedies with us shows the opposite."

Zach frowned in disagreement. "You make Him sound like He's powerless to stop it in the first place."

Laina moved to a grassy spot on the bank to their right not far from the pool's overflow. She set her pack down and began to rig her line. Zach dropped his pack and sat beside her, all the while wondering why she did not answer. The silence stretched for at least five minutes when finally she spoke.

"God isn't powerless to stop the bad things that happen in our lives. First I think you need to understand that sickness and evil were not a part of His creation. The moment man sinned back in the Garden of Eden, sickness came into the world and so did death. You also need to understand that a lot of the bad things that happen in this world are the result of people's misuse of their free will.

"God gave mankind the will to love and obey Him, or to hate and reject Him. Unfortunately a lot of people make bad choices that impact negatively upon those around them. God won't remove people's choice to do evil, because in doing so he would also be removing their choice to do good. We all have choices. Choices to love God and make wise loving decisions, choices to hate or to live selfishly, and choices over what attitude we will take when faced with the awful consequences of other men's actions." Laina's thoughtful gaze followed the line she was casting into the stream.

She did not look at Zach. If she had she would have seen anger hardening his eyes.

"That's just a bunch of religious rubbish! You wouldn't say all that if you'd watched your own father die and listened to his chest rattle as he fought for his last breath." Zach's anguish rose to the surface and with it those agonizing memories.

He saw her glance at his profile from his peripheral vision. His jaw muscles tensed as he worked to control the anger bubbling within him. His hard, pain-filled gaze stared out over the water, seeing nothing.

"You're wrong, Zach," she replied softly, "so very wrong." She returned her focus to the float bobbing up and down in the current. "My dad died in a car accident and I was sitting right next to him."

Zach's gaze swung to meet hers in surprise. "I didn't know," he offered by way of apology. His anger quickly drained away.

"There's a lot you don't know about me. I'm not saying you don't have a legitimate right to grieve. I'm just saying that you're not the only one to have suffered."

Zach broke eye contact and both teenagers studied the river. "How did it happen?"

"An eighteen wheeler ran a red light. Dad had nowhere to go and it was coming at my side of the vehicle. He turned the wheel sharply but the truck clipped the tail of our car. It spun us straight into its path on his side. I still feel bad about that." Laina's voice shook and tears blurred her vision. "It should have been me who died, not him. I used to wish sometimes that it was me."

Zach studied her, for the first time glimpsing the sorrow in her soul. Something inside of him broke over her suffering. She was right. He had been acting selfishly. "When did it happen?"

"Three years ago."

"How did your mum take it?" Zach remembered his own mother's grief. The days and weeks and months of tears, the broken prayers that had fallen from her lips. That had been just as hard to deal with as the death of his father.

"My mother died when I was born."

"You're an orphan? Who do you live with?" She had to have a very supportive family to be so well adjusted.

"No one really. I'm supposed to be living with my uncle, but he's not exactly the nicest person in the world. So I pretty much come and go as I please. I guess that's why I get upset with the way you treat your mom. I know you're angry with her for moving you here, but you should at least be grateful that you have her at all. What I wouldn't give to have what you've got."

Zach hated to admit it, but she was right. Suddenly he saw his own life in a different light. It may not have turned out the way he wanted, but he certainly hadn't lost as much as Laina had.

"I'm sorry for being an idiot."

"Believe me, I understand how you're feeling. I've been there. Just please don't take it out on those around you. They're the ones that need your support the most."

"I'll try," Zach offered sincerely, realizing for the first time in months that he needed to make a change.

He couldn't go on being angry at the world. It was making him miserable and it was hurting his mom. Although he hated being held accountable, he could not argue when it was done with kindness and compassion.

The float disappeared beneath the surface and Laina's rod bent nearly double. She came to her feet and began to fight a tenacious, wily trout. Zach shouted encouragement and watched as she landed the enormous fish.

"Would you look at that! He's gotta be the great granddaddy of them all!"

"I reckon!"

Laina removed the hook from its mouth, dealt the death blow, and stored the fish in a small foldable mesh trap that she took from her pack. It was attached to a string by which she let the trap down into the cool mountain water to keep chilled.

She grinned. "Alright Zach, it's your turn."

He smiled eagerly in return and baited the hook. The conversation turned to lighter topics and over the next hour the pair caught several more fish. The sun beat mercilessly down upon their heads and both broke into a sweat. Deciding they had caught enough trout for a feast that evening, they called it quits.

"Come with me, Zach," Laina beckoned with an adventurous gleam in her eyes.

"Where are we going?" He followed her along the water's edge, climbing higher and higher toward the waterfall.

They were near the top on the left rock wall, the waterfall only five yards away, staring down over the sheer drop into the deep, crystal clear pool below. Without warning Laina gave a laugh and leapt out into thin air. With a delighted whoop she plummeted fully clothed into the water with an almighty splash.

Zach thought she was insane. What if she broke a leg? Then he remembered that she had been here many times before.

Laina surfaced grinning from ear to ear. "It's beautiful in here!"

Zach hesitated. "Are you sure it's deep enough to just jump in? Television commercials warn about doing stuff like that. They say you should check the depth of the water first."

"You couldn't hit the bottom even if you had cement tied to your feet. It goes clear to China."

"That's a slight exaggeration."

"Come on! What are you waiting for?" She trod water in the center of the pool.

Zach took a deep breath and dredged up the courage to jump. "Don't do this at home kids!" He leapt, screaming the whole way.

Laina laughed as he came crashing down. He disappeared beneath the surface for several seconds before coming up for breath.

"Wow!" His face wreathed in a huge smile. "You were right. This thing is deep. I couldn't even see the bottom when I was down there."

"I told you so. Do you want to go again?" She was ready for another thrill.

"Nope. I want to see what's behind that waterfall. From here it looks like a cavern."

Laina grinned. "It is. You should see the falls from inside."

Zach smiled broadly with the excitement of an adventure. "Let's go."

~

Dripping wet and laden with their catches of the day, Laina and Zach headed home late that afternoon. They were almost to the ravine when Zach paused with his head cocked to one side. Noticing that she was striding ahead alone, Laina stopped and turned around. He seemed to be listening intently.

"What is it?"

"I don't know. Can you hear it?"

Laina was puzzled. "Hear what?"

"That strange whirring sound." Zach's eyes scanned the forest around them. All that was visible were towering trees of all varieties and low shrubbery.

"Come to think of it, I *can* hear something weird. It sounds mechanical. I think it's coming from that direction." She pointed behind and to their right. "Let's check it out."

"Alright, but we'll leave our stuff here." Zach shrugged off his pack and hung his string of fish on a branch.

Laina did the same. They set off together, weaving through massive trunks of old forest growth on stealthy feet. Not ten yards from where they had left their packs, a strange aroma greeted Laina's senses. Then she spotted it. Another three paces away was what appeared to be a deer carcass. They made a careful approach.

"It looks dead."

"Well it's not." Laina knelt beside it and inspected its brown fur coat for a bullet hole or any kind of puncture mark. None. Its large chest rose and fell in a shallow but steady rhythm. She marveled. "It's sleeping."

"Then why doesn't it wake up?" Zach nudged a hoof with his shoe.

The animal did not even stir.

"And what's that smell?" Laina wrinkled her nose at the unusual odor lingering in the air. "It's stronger around the deer."

"I don't know, but it's making me feel strange." He forced suddenly drowsy eyelids to stay open.

"Hey, that weird sound is gone." Laina rose to her feet. Her head was starting to throb. "I don't feel so good either. Let's get out of here."

They stumbled away. Laina felt worse for every second she had spent near the animal. The further away she got and the more fresh air she inhaled, the better she started to feel. They collected their gear and hightailed it out of the woods. Laina was more than a little spooked.

~

"This is quite a feast." Caroline beamed at the two teenagers sitting around the small circular dining table that evening.

In the center was a plate filled with battered and fried fillets of fish. To compliment the fish was another plate piled high with homemade fries. Laina and Zach grinned at one another, clearly pleased with their day's work.

"Let's thank the Lord for this food and get stuck into it." Caroline bowed her head to pray.

Laina followed her lead, however Zach kept his eyes open in silent refusal.

"Lord, we thank You for providing for us so bountifully. These fish look delicious. We're grateful for our new friend Laina and that she and Zach had a wonderful day. Thank You for keeping them safe. We pray in Your name." Caroline lifted her head and grinned. "Dig in!"

As they ate, Zach enthusiastically expounded on their exploits in greater detail. Caroline's countenance lifted as she listened to her previously despondent son regale her with tales of courage and intrigue.

He could not wipe the smile off his face. Laina did not miss Caroline's encouragement of their friend-ship with gentle nudges during the conversation, and supposed there must be some big changes evident to her in Zach since their move. A little adventure and a whole lot of God's love were always a good recipe for healing.

7

"Good morning Deputy," Laina greeted Dan Fisher Monday morning. She crossed his path on her way to deliver a steaming plate of eggs, bacon and sausage to a waiting customer.

"Good morning Laina." He gave her a chipper smile. "Hey, when you're done with that tray, would you take my order?"

"Sure thing, but if you're in a hurry, Candice has a spare moment."

"No, I want you." Dan moseyed at a leisurely pace to a table by the window overlooking the main street of Icy Creek.

Laina raised curious brows and then shrugged. She delivered the meal before sashaying back to the table where the deputy was patiently waiting. "What can I do for you, Mr. Fisher?"

"It's Dan, Laina, you know that."

"I know, but it always seems a little disrespectful when you're in uniform." She smiled amiably.

Dan chuckled and his eyes lit with amusement.

"You're a good girl, Laina Jackson."

Laina waited patiently for the deputy to speak his mind, her expression curious. Dan noted her attentiveness and got straight to the point.

"A couple of the computers at the station are playing up. I wanted to give your uncle a call to see if he might drop in and take a look at them, but when I tried his business number in Walkerville, the receptionist said he no longer works there."

Laina's brows winged upward. "That's weird. I guess he's got a new job."

"So you didn't know about it either? I was hoping you'd be able to give me his new business number." Dan frowned with curiosity. "How is it, Laina, that you live under the same roof as your uncle and yet you had no idea that he hasn't been working in Walkerville for at least a year?"

Laina felt her face drain of color. She couldn't lie yet neither could she divulge her situation. To do so would mean one of two things. She might be rebuked for misrepresenting her uncle, or she could be removed from the town she called home and placed in the welfare system.

Besides, Dan Fisher had great respect for Rylan. Her friendship with Allie had taught her not to combat the power of her uncle's charm and the beguiling impressions he left with the townsfolk. She had once made the mistake of telling Allie the full truth about Rylan, only to have her friend refuse to believe her and publicly humiliate her by blabbing it all over school.

She had been confronted by several upset and angry townspeople, demanding an answer to why she would make up such lies about the kind, wonderful man that had so graciously taken her in. That had ended her friendship with Allie.

Fortunately for her, Dan shook his head in dismay and smiled. "Teenagers today! They've no time for older folks."

Laina breathed a sigh of relief and smiled. "Sorry I can't help you."

Dan waved her apology aside. "That's all right. I might stop by the house tonight and see him in person."

"Sounds like a good plan. So, what can I get you?" Laina brandished her note pad and pencil.

"Just a cup of coffee and a donut."

"Coming right up." Laina was never more grateful to head toward the kitchen than at that moment.

~

Laina had just knocked off work that same afternoon when three familiar faces entered the diner and took their regular corner table. They spread a map between them and their heads bent to study it. Their voices were conspiratorially low and Laina was intrigued.

She removed her apron and tossed it on a chair in the kitchen. She left her note pad and pencil on the counter by the cash register and wandered over to see what Nick, Wil and Logan were up to. They saw her approaching and hastily refolded the map. Laina could not suppress a cheeky smile.

"Trying to hide a good fishing spot boys?"

"You bet ya," Logan retorted a little too quickly.

Laina frowned in puzzlement, realizing then that this had nothing to do with fishing. She slid into the booth beside Nick uninvited.

"What are you up to? And don't give me any rubbish about fishing spots. You're all looking mighty secretive and I want to know what's going on."

Logan rolled his eyes and sat back against the booth, releasing an impatient breath. Nick stared at Laina with a reluctant expression while Wil glanced uncertainly from one face to another.

"You're obviously planning to rob the Icy Creek bank," she cajoled, "and I want in."

Wil snorted and broke into sudden laughter which made Laina smile in pure enjoyment.

"Oh come on guys, let me in on whatever you're up

to? I could do with an adventure after my mundane day."

Nick looked to Logan and raised a questioning brow. Logan shook his head adamantly in silent answer.

"She spends time up there too, Logan. She might have seen some stuff like we did."

"Would you keep shut already!"

Laina remembered the mysterious whirring sound and the comatose deer. Had they seen something equally mystifying while on their fishing trip? She eagerly sat forward, leaning her elbows on the table. "You've noticed strange stuff going on up there too, haven't you?"

This brought the three boys to attention.

Logan studied her speculatively. "What did you see?"

All three trained keen eyes upon her. She launched into a brief explanation of what she and Zach had encountered. "It was weird," she concluded. "It was like the animal had been drugged, but there was no mark on it. And that smell... It made me and Zach feel strange, almost like we would pass out if we hung around too long."

Nick was intrigued. "What do you think the whirring sound was?"

Laina stared into thin air pensively, her mind conjuring up the memory of that foreign noise. "It was definitely mechanical, but soft. I can't explain it any other way. You'd have to hear it yourself to under-stand that it's not like anything you would've ever heard before." She looked at each of the guys around the table. "Alright, I've told you what I know. What did you see?"

Although Logan still appeared reluctant to share, Nick had no such reservations. He explained in detail their hike between fishing holes, the terrain and their rough location. "We crept to the top of a rise and saw two guys lifting a heavy case. We didn't get a look at what was in it, but I'll bet whatever it is, it makes a whirring sound. They were talking about finding out the cause of a power drainage. But check this, we got Wil's uncle Dan to look up their license plate. It was a government truck."

"I'll bet someone's making some kind of secret invention that they've been testing out there where they hope no one will find out about it," Logan sur-mised.

Laina grinned and waggled her eyebrows mischie-vously. "There's only one way to find out."

~

"I can't believe you let her bring this loser along,"

Logan grumbled as the five teenagers began their hike into the untamed wilderness on the outskirts of Icy Creek.

"He was with Laina when they found that deer. We need him. Besides, Zach's a decent guy. You should give him a chance." Nick met Zach's gaze as they walked.

Logan's hostile eyes bored directly into Zach's. "I ain't givin' no city slicker a chance. I wish you'd just go back to where you came from."

Zach silently fumed.

Laina had to take large strides to keep up with the tall young men following the forest trail deeper into the woods. "I was a city slicker and I'm not so bad."

"You're as big a pain as he is."

Laina puzzled over Logan's irritation with her. That his gaze passed between Zach and her again made her wonder if he was jealous of their friendship. She quickly dismissed the bizarre notion.

"You know, you can be really nice when you try to be, but when you're acting like this you're a real drag." Laina immediately felt guilty for her lack of graciousness and knew she would have to apologize. "I'm sorry Logan, that was nasty."

Logan glanced back at her in surprise. It appeared no one ever apologized to him. He focused on the trail ahead.

"Whatever."

Wil said nothing, but the apologetic glance he sent Zach's way made the newcomer look a little more at ease. Logan seemed to be the only one with a grudge against him.

~

They reached the ravine and all five crossed the log confidently. Zach found himself enjoying the beauty around him and especially the thrill of a real adventure. The lure of the city paled in comparison to the excitement of a genuine mystery to solve.

"Alright," Laina broke the companionable silence, "it was near here, just off to the right." She pointed and started in that direction.

Zach walked beside her while the others followed close behind.

"There." Zach indicated a tall spruce. "It was lying near that tree."

"Yeah, you're right."

"Well it's gone now." Nick's eyes scanned the surrounding terrain.

It was rocky in places, but for the most part green and fertile. Large trees of all varieties stretched toward the heavens. They were spaced well apart, giving plenty of room for the bushy undergrowth

that was sprouting. Wild flowers popped their color-
ful heads above the ground, bobbing gleefully in the
gentle breeze.

Everything was quiet and tranquil. The refreshing
aroma of earth and vegetation greeted Zach's senses.
Gone was the strange odor that had lingered in the
air only a few days ago.

Logan carefully studied the area. "I still think we
should find that logging track where we saw those
two men. It's far more accessible by car than the forest up here."

Laina met his gaze inquiringly. "How long will it
take us to hike there?"

"Till lunchtime at least," Wil spoke up for the first
time that morning.

Laina shrugged. "It's worth a try."

"Besides, some open fields are near there. You
know, the ones at the base of the Tanner Ranges,"
Nick added. "Those meadows are surrounded by
forest. They're the perfect place if someone really is
testing something."

Zach marveled at the vast knowledge these teenagers had of the land. They seemed to know every
nook and cranny. He smiled wryly to himself, suppos-
ing that not having a skate park or a shopping mall
had something to do with it.

"I think you're right," Logan agreed.

Zach liked the idea. "Let's get started then."
In minutes the team was on their way.

~

"There's the logging track the government truck used." Logan indicated a rocky dirt road winding into the forest on the other side of a small meadow. It had taken an hour longer than Wil had predicted to reach this spot.

"Now what?" Zach was feeling well baked by the hot summer sun.

Nick was pragmatic. "I guess we follow it and see where it leads."

"I vote we find the creek and have a swim." Zach removed his pack and flopped wearily into a shady patch of grass beneath a large oak on the edge of the clearing.

"That's a brilliant idea." Laina stretched out in the grass beside him.

Wil wordlessly dropped his pack and headed toward an enormous spruce on the opposite edge of the meadow. At its base he bent his knees and made a huge leap. His hands latched onto a thick branch and he swung his legs up, disappearing into dense foliage.

Logan looked perplexed. "What are you doing

Wil?"

"Trying to get a bird's eye view." His voice came from a quarter of the way up the tree, surprising his friends with the speed at which he was climbing.

"Great idea!" Nick grinned and jogged to the base of the spruce. In minutes he too was concealed within the shelter of its branches.

"It sure is stinking hot today!" Zach wiped sweat from his brow.

"Tell me about it!" Laina closed tired eyes and appeared ready to take a catnap.

"Would you two quit whining?" Logan's surly growl carried easily on the gentle afternoon breeze.

Zach lifted himself up on his elbows and glared at his rival. "You know, I've had just about enough of you. You've done nothing but pick on us all day. What's your problem?"

Laina sat up and placed a restraining hand on his forearm. "Zach, please don't? Just drop it."

Zach looked at her sitting beside him. The combination of Logan's antagonism, the simmering heat, and Laina's irritating penchant for preserving the peace, squeezed the last ounce of tolerance out of him.

Logan took a swig from his canteen. He wiped his damp mouth on his arm. "You're my problem. I thought I made that clear from day one."

"That does it!" Zach sprang to his feet and strode purposefully toward his adversary.

Laina rolled her eyes and groaned. "That's right," she raised her voice sarcastically, "beat each other up till you're bruised, broken and bleeding! It'll provide a little entertainment."

Zach was just reaching for Logan's collar with his left while drawing back his right to strike, when Wil called down from the top of the tree.

"Hey, I can see something in the distance!"

Nick was unable to see from his position slightly below Wil. "What is it?"

"A shiny roof in the middle of the forest."

"A shed?"

"No, it's big." Wil's voice drifted down to the three onlookers in the meadow. "I think it's some kind of factory."

Logan pushed Zach away with a scathing glare, and Zach pushed back. Several twigs snapped near the top of the tree as Nick ascended quickly. Finally he could be seen perching on a branch next to Wil, peering through a gap in the bushy pine needles. "I see it too." Nick studied the iron roof gleaming in the afternoon sun, nestled securely in the midst of a blanket of trees.

Zach and Logan cast a final withering glance at one another before shifting their attention to the top of the spruce which Wil and Nick were using as a look-out.

"How far away is it?" Logan's hands went to his hips and his eyes lifted to the top of the tree.

"About ten miles," Nick estimated.

Zach's brows arched in surprise. "That's not far. We could walk that in half a day, maybe less."

Logan's mind had turned to plotting and planning, his altercation with Zach momentarily forgotten. "We can't get there today or we'd be walking home in the dark."

"We could camp over."

Both Logan and Zach glanced at Laina with expressions that said she had taken leave of her senses. They had families who were expecting them home tonight. Other than work at the diner tomorrow afternoon, Laina was pretty much a free agent.

"Maybe in a day or so," she amended.

"Hey guys!" Nick sounded alarmed. "I can see something coming toward us in the trees. I can't see what it is but it's moving fast."

Laina rose to her feet, her wary gaze scanning the forest surrounding the meadow for any sign of an approaching threat. "From which direction?"

"Dead ahead, from the factory. Whatever it is, it's close." Wil focused on the small shadow darting between trees at a frightening speed.

Laina backed toward the boys, dwarfed by their towering frames. Before any of them could do a thing, what appeared to be a small, sleek black glider no greater in wing span than a yard, hurtled from the trees at the edge of the clearing. It sped straight for them making a strange whirring sound.

"What in the..."

Logan did not even have time to finish his cry of bewilderment before the flying object whooshed past them, discharging some kind of gas from its undercarriage.

Zach recognized the odor seconds before all three succumbed to its intoxicating power.

~

Nick and Wil watched helplessly from their perch as their three friends slumped to the ground, unconscious even before they landed on the grass.

"What was that?"

The black object re-entered the clearing and hovered above the comatose teens. If Nick didn't know better, he would have sworn it was studying them. Suddenly it shifted course, flying directly toward the spruce as though it knew exactly where they were hiding. Panic seized hold of him and he started to scramble back down.

"Hang on, Nick." Wil plucked several pinecones from the branch above his head and aimed them at the mysterious device now only two yards away. He let loose the first pinecone which skimmed off the smooth exterior. The second hit dead on. The combination of the object's speed and the force with which Wil hurled the solid pinecone, sent the device into a downward spiral. Nick paused as he watched it lose its stability.

"Good shot!"

However, the machine stopped its out of control descent and hovered for several seconds, reminding Nick of a professional boxer regaining his senses after receiving a blow to the head. Wil quickly snatched three more pinecones in preparation for the attack that was coming. Nick did likewise.

Sure enough, it propelled itself upward, ready to take them on again. It drew to within three yards and they launched their arsenal. One of Nick's missed and the other found its mark with lethal force, along with each of Wil's. The machine made a sickening electrical fizzling sound and then went into a death spin, finally landing on the ground with a thud.

Nick and Wil exchanged anxious glances. Was that it? Or would it recover again? They watched silently for several minutes. It did not move. They had won this round. Nick would have laughed in triumph had it not been for his friends lying prone in the middle of the small meadow.

"Do you think they're dead?" Wil asked the horrifying question on both of their minds.

"Let's get there fast." Nick scrambled down as quickly as his arms and legs could safely carry him.

Wil followed. They were halfway when the sound of a vehicle drifted through the forest.

"Someone's coming." Wil stopped climbing to listen. "Can you hear that? It's a pickup truck."

Nick looked at his friend in amazement. All he could hear was a distant engine. Distinguishing what kind of engine it was at this point was beyond his ability. They listened for another moment. The vehicle was travelling at a high speed. It would arrive in minutes. They would not have enough time to get their friends out of there. They would manage only to get caught. Then what help could they offer?

"Do you think the pickup's travelling from the factory?" Nick wondered aloud.

"No. Whoever it is, they were close by, probably monitoring that thing we just trashed."

Nick grimaced. "They're gonna be mad."

"We're the ones that should be mad. It just tried to gas us. What if we had blacked out while up this tree? We'd be dead for sure."

"Do you think they'll be alright?" Nick's stomach

churned sickeningly.

"I hope so. You *have* realized we can't go down there. Besides the truck, that gas won't have cleared yet. Remember what Laina and Zach described when they found that deer? I think the deer was gassed by whatever that is."

The sound of an engine at full throttle disturbed the unnatural silence. It drew closer and grew louder. Finally a black pickup sped along the logging track into the clearing and ground to a halt in a cloud of dust. Wil and Nick glanced at each other and sank further into the safety of the spruce's thick foliage.

"Oh you have got to be kidding!" an angry male voice roared as the stranger climbed out of the vehicle. "It's taken out a bunch of kids! I thought you said this thing could distinguish between human and animal!" A man in his thirties, with wildly curly black hair and a powerful build, reached into the vehicle and donned a gas mask. He stormed toward the comatose teenagers.

"It can. I didn't think anyone would be out here on a weekday so I left it on human detection mode." An older man also pulled a gas mask over his mouth and nose. His thinning brown hair was styled into a comb over.

Wil and Nick stared at one another, eyes wide in recognition. It was the same two men they had seen on their fishing trip. The pair silently studied the men now crouched beside their friends, feeling for pulses and listening for breathing.

"They're alive," the younger man stated with relief, his voice sounding slightly muffled with the mask on.

"What did you expect? It was on seek, not on destroy."

"Where is it by the way?" The younger man stood and surveyed the clearing.

From what Nick could see of his face, he appeared to be frowning.

"What are we supposed to do with them now? They've seen the hawk! This will totally blow our anonymity. What a mess!"

"The hawk?" Nick repeated the name quietly under his breath. They had named that menace of a machine after a bird of prey.

The older gentleman stood and stared at his partner, whose back was to him. "You're making a mountain out of a molehill. We'll simply drop them off near Icy Creek, seeing as it's the closest town, and they'll come to in a matter of hours. They'll run on home with an incredible tale, which no one will believe, and we'll continue our business at Astro Enterprises. It's not as grim as you make it out to be."

"Isn't it?" The other man raised one eyebrow and glanced back at his workmate. He pointed to something beneath a tall pine. "I think the situation just got worse. There's H5-40."

The older gentleman left the unlucky hikers and went to investigate the black triangular shaped glider lying lifeless in the grass near a spruce. Both men bent down to inspect the damage.

"It's dented. Do you suppose it ran into a tree?"

The younger fellow smiled mirthlessly. He indicated several pinecones scattered about. "I'd say those kids got off a few shots before H5-40 took them out."

Nick held his breath, desperately hoping the strangers would stick with that conclusion, even though it made more sense that there was someone else nearer the tree.

The older man sighed in defeat. "Oh well, we'd better drop these kids off and get H5-40 back to the lab."

"Come on, I'll give you a hand lifting this hunk of junk."

In the nerve-racking minutes that followed, Nick and Wil watched the strangers load the device into the back seat of the truck. Then they carried Logan, Zach and Laina one by one and laid them in the vehicle's tray. Beside them they tossed the kids' packs.

They climbed into the pickup and the engine roared to life. The two boys up the tree watched helplessly as the vehicle carrying their friends disappeared down the logging track, heading toward Icy

Creek. Once the pickup was out of sight, they came down from their hiding place. They looked at the dirt road, over which a cloud of dust was settling, and then at one another.

"Let's get out of here," Wil urged.

"I'm with you."

They set out for town as fast as they could travel on foot in the blistering heat.

8

Dry twigs and leaves crunched beneath Laina as she roused and shifted. She groaned and rolled onto her back. Her limbs felt as though they were made of lead. She slowly opened her eyes and squinted to see beyond the shaft of sunlight in her face. Leaves within the treetops high above her were tickled by a gentle breeze. She frowned. What was she doing lying on the forest floor?

She slowly sat up and looked about in a daze. From the corner of her eye she caught a glimpse of a pair of shoes. She turned her head for a better view and panic hit her like a blow to the stomach. Those were Zach's runners and he was sprawled face down in the dirt, unconscious.

Near him Logan also lay prone. She tried to stand but found that she did not have the strength. She settled for crawling to Zach's side on her hands and knees. She grasped his shoulder and shook him. He groaned but did not awaken.

"Zach, wake up!"

He mumbled and his legs moved several inches, then he lay still again. Laina moved on to Logan. He was also lying face down, his head turned to one side and his cheek pressing against several small twigs and a bed of leaves. She shook his shoulder. He drew in a deep breath and opened heavy eyelids. He blinked several times before focusing upon the face staring anxiously into his own.

"Logan, are you okay?"

"Yeah, I suppose. Where are we?" He pulled himself onto his hands and knees and then sat, his legs stretched before him. He shook his head as if trying to dispel the haze clouding his thoughts. Then he spotted Zach. "Is he alright?"

Laina crawled back to her friend and shook him again. "I don't know."

Zach groaned and slowly awakened. His confused gaze drifted over his strange surroundings. A now familiar odor tainted their clothing.

"It got us." His voice was husky from lack of use. He rolled onto his back and squinted up at the leafy canopy far above them.

"You mean that flying black thing?" Logan attempted to stand on wobbly legs. He ended up doubled over with his hands on his knees for balance.

With each deep breath, Laina felt her head gradually clearing. She held onto a nearby sapling and pulled herself to her feet. "Do you remember how fast it came at us?"

"Yeah. What do you suppose it is?" Zach struggled to his feet as well.

"I don't know, but what I'm more worried about is how we got here and where Wil and Nick are," Logan replied.

"Where are we?" Zach stared about at the forest towering over them, dappled by shafts of late afternoon sunshine penetrating its protective canopy. Nearby, a dirt track wound through the trees.

"We're close to town. That road takes us into Icy Creek," Laina enlightened him.

"How did we get here?"

Logan collected his pack from where it had been haphazardly tossed. "I've got no idea. All I know is we'd better get to the sheriff's office and report this. Maybe he can help us find Wil and Nick?"

Laina and Zach exchanged worried glances and followed Logan's lead.

~

The five teenagers strolled down the main street of Icy Creek over two hours later.

Logan, Zach and Laina had hurried to the sheriff's office only to find Wil and Nick already there. Both were in a panic and were desperately trying to convince Wil's uncle and Sheriff Hawkins to get a search party together to find their missing friends.

Upon their arrival, Deputy Fisher lost his patience for the tale telling group. He and the sheriff were then called to a domestic disturbance, leaving the teens standing in his office frustrated and dejected by their offhand dismissal.

They had gone to Gracie's Diner for a bite to eat and a chance to chew over their discovery and plan a fresh line of attack. Having resolved to set out on Friday by bike, they had left the diner and started to mosey on home.

A fancy red sports car pulled to the curb alongside the group and a tinted electric window lowered. Laina's heart sank and her nerves grew taut. The handsome blond haired, blue-eyed driver gave the teens a winsome smile.

"Good afternoon gentleman," he greeted politely and nodded. "Laina, jump in. I'll give you a ride home."

"Thanks for the offer, Uncle Rylan, but I'll be alright." She wondered why he was suddenly seeking her out. Dread filled her.

"Why are you saying no to a ride in that?" Nick teased, open admiration written across his face as he appreciated the smooth sleek design of the sports car. He appeared to be one step away from lovingly caressing the vehicle.

"It's not a request, honey." Rylan's look was apologetic. "I need your help with dinner tonight."

Laina knew he would put on a nice face in front of her friends, but when he got her home... She debated saying no straight out, but concluded it would only lead to more trouble later. Against her better judgment, she decided to play along.

"I'll see you tomorrow, guys." She got into the car.

Rylan waved to the boys with his charming smile in place.

"Bye Mr. Jackson," Nick called, his usual amiable smile in place.

Wil waved and Logan gave a short nod of acknowledgement. A curious crease found Zach's brow.

With a deep burble the engine revved and the car cruised down the street out of sight.

~

"So," Rylan began as soon as they pulled away from the curb, "where've you been for the last two months?" He sounded casual, but Laina knew better.

"School and work."

Her gaze drifted out the window. She felt his eyes on her and returned his stare. He looked so much like her father, however appearance was where the likeness ended. His eyes were smoldering angrily.

"Where do you work?"

"I thought I told you." Laina kept her voice calm and her manner laid-back, although beneath the facade she was apprehensive.

"Enlighten me again." This time his tone held a distinct bite.

"I work at Gracie's Diner. Uncle Rylan, where are you working at the moment?" She was genuinely interested, and did her best to ignore the irate tensing of his jaw muscles.

"None of your business."

"It's just that Deputy Fisher was asking the other day. He was having a computer problem at the office and rang your old workplace. He said they told him you hadn't been there for a long time. I was just curious. I figured you must have gotten a better offer. I know you're very good at what you do." Laina's attempt at civil conversation fell flat.

"Drop the act. You're in deep strife." His hard gaze fell upon her and then refocused on the road. They were nearly home.

"I can't imagine what for. I've worked my backside off at school and I'm a good employee at Gracie's. I don't ask you for a thing. Why are you angry?"

"Because you were born." Rylan's expression darkened with malice and he drove into his driveway. He put the car in park and turned to look at her.

Laina stared at him, shocked by his vindictive answer. She could not fathom why he hated her so passionately.

Please God, get me away from this man?

"You've been traipsing through the wilderness causing trouble and I'm telling you it stops today."

Laina frowned in bewilderment. How did he know about her fishing adventures? Had he bumped into one of her friends at another time? "What do you mean?"

"I'm talking about your little escapade today." Rylan's stare was meaningful.

How did he know about that? Her mind quickly made a few suppositions. Did he have something to do with that machine?

"What escapade?" She wanted him to come straight out and say it.

"You know what I'm referring to so stop playing innocent. I don't care what you do or even if you never come home again, but stay out of those woods. It's my final warning." His cold tone sent a chill down her spine.

She was astonished. "Is that a threat?"

Rylan's hostile eyes bored into hers. "Take it however you want. Just know that next time there will be consequences."

Laina wanted to run, yet for the sake of their mission, she pushed for more information. "Are you a part of the H5-40 project?"

Rylan's reaction was instant. His hand shot out and grasped her wrist like a vice, cutting off the blood supply. Laina jumped with fright and tried to pull away. It was futile. He was too strong. His free hand grabbed her throat and she gasped for breath, petrified beyond belief.

With his incensed face inches from hers, his eyes burning with rage, he gritted out between clenched teeth, "You had better forget that name, for your own sake!" He shoved her away and her head bumped the passenger window.

She scrambled for the door handle, wrenched it open and tumbled from the vehicle. As soon as her feet touched the paved driveway, she bolted. Once on the footpath, she sprinted for the track that led to her tree house. Her lungs were burning and tears stung her eyes but she kept going, leaping over tree roots protruding from the ground and brushing past foliage on the narrow track through the woods.

She reached the large oak tree and climbed into the welcome safe haven of her home, bolting the door shut behind her. She told herself that Rylan had not followed, but fear would not let her rest at ease.

He had struck her before, yet never had he choked her and made her fear for her life.

She drew her knees up to her chest and wrapped her arms around them, her back to the cubby wall. Her tears came in earnest then and did not stop for quite some time.

9

Laina was too afraid to venture out the next day. She did something unprecedented and skipped work without a word of explanation. She stayed safely ensconced in her tree house, deeply anxious about what to do next.

After much prayer and thought, she concluded that it wasn't worth the trouble she would get into to find out more about H5-40. She feared for the boys. What would happen to them if they persisted? She decided to pay Logan a visit. He was the ringleader. If he dropped it, the others would too.

Despite the gnawing fear that she might bump into Rylan again, Laina headed across town on foot just after dusk. At first the darkness cloaked her and she felt a little more secure. Then she reached lamp lit streets and her eyes warily scanned every shadow for possible dangers.

Finally she strode down the ghost street where Logan lived. She entered the small, well kept yard and with another quick glance behind her, went to the front door and softly knocked. There was no movement within and so Laina backtracked a few steps to peer through the living room window.

Light spilled from the room into the yard. The scene inside was similar to the one she had shown Zach not long ago. Mrs. Mathews was fast asleep in a worn recliner and Logan's younger sister was seated on the couch ripping small bits off a Kleenex, twisting them in her fingers and then dropping them. She watched them twirl to the floor with great fascination. That particular patch of carpet was littered with tissue pieces and Laina could not resist a smile. If Mrs. Mathews or Logan were aware of what she was doing for entertainment, she was certain they would put a stop to it.

Logan entered the room and spotted the small mountain of tissue pieces piling ever higher. Laina did not wait to see his reaction. She quickly went to the front door and knocked again. Footsteps sounded in the entrance and the door opened a crack.

"Who is it and what do you want?" Logan snapped warily.

There was no light over the doorway, for which Laina was grateful. She preferred the safety of darkness. "It's me."

Logan opened the door wider. "What are you doing here?" He sounded puzzled, and thankfully not hostile.

"I need to talk to you."

"Sure, come in." His expression was a mixture of curiosity and surprise.

"Can you come out?"

Logan frowned in bewilderment. "Okay." He stepped onto the front stoop and closed the door behind him. "What's wrong?" He squinted into the darkness to see her face. Laina was certain all he could make out was a vague outline.

"I'm not going with you to check out the factory."

"Alright," he answered slowly. "Any particular reason you walked across town in the dark just to tell me that?"

"I don't want you to go either. The others will want to but they won't if you decide it's not a good idea. They follow you Logan. Please don't go?"

"Why not?"

"Just please, don't go?" Laina was unable to mask the fear in her voice.

"You're not still spooked by today are you? 'Cause if you are you shouldn't be. It'll take those men a while to fix that thing after what Wil and Nick did to it."

"It's not that."

Logan appeared both worried and confused. "Then what is it?"

"It's not safe. That's all I can say right now. Don't go, I'm begging you?"

Logan took a step toward her and she automatically backed away several paces down the footpath, inadvertently stepping into the light pouring from the living room window. His horrified gaze rested upon the black bruises on her left wrist and the finger marks around her throat.

"Where did those bruises come from?" His intense stare penetrated her frightened gaze, reading more than she was willing to share.

"Just don't go!" She was angry at herself for her inability to stop the tears that pooled in her eyes.

Logan tried to approach her and she backed away again. "I'm not going to hurt you, but I'll wring the neck of whoever did!"

"This thing is bigger than us and if we keep poking around who knows what will happen next?"

"Someone threatened you, didn't they?" It was more a statement than a question. Understanding chased across his features followed by shock at who was responsible. "It was your uncle. Those old rumors Allie started were true."

Laina was speechless. She had longed for someone to believe her, to know and understand. On the other hand, she wanted it kept a secret. The shame, the humiliation, the pain... Those were not things she wanted others to see. Her face crumpled miserably and she turned and fled.

~

Logan watched her go in stunned paralysis. He ran a hand through his hair and blew out his cheeks. The last thing he wanted was to put her in jeopardy. Clearly their situation had become more complicated than he first thought. He needed to get the guys together. However, before he could do that he needed more information from Laina. The mystery had taken an unexpected twist.

~

"Gracie." Logan approached the cash register where the proprietor was counting the day's takings. "Have you seen Laina?"

Gracie took several more seconds to finish the tally, write down the total and bag the cash. Finally she glanced up at the teenager waiting impatiently for an answer.

"No, Logan, I ain't seen 'er. Which is totally out o' the ordinary if ya ask me. Laina ain't missed one day o' work in a year." Worry furrowed her brow. "Now she's missed two. Why? Is there somethin' goin' on I don't know about?"

Logan debated sharing her situation. He knew that Laina and Gracie were good friends. On the other hand, he also understood how Laina was feeling right now. Having been mistreated in the past, he was well acquainted with the baggage that went along with it. She would not want people talking about her.

"She wasn't feeling well yesterday." Logan was as discreet as he could be. "Oh well, I might stop by her house. Bye Gracie." He waved and exited before the concerned woman could stop him with the questions he read in her eyes.

Next he tried the Jackson mansion. No one was home. Having no other recourse, he reluctantly made his way over to Zach Delaney's house. Maybe he would know where to locate Laina.

Logan knocked on the front door and waited. Hurried footsteps click clacked down the hall and the door was wrenched open. A blond woman, probably in her early forties, with kind brown eyes held the door with one hand and her purse and keys in the other. Although looking a little harried, her smile was warm and welcoming.

"Hi, you must be one of Zach's friends. Come on in."

"Name's Logan. Is Zach around?" Logan felt terribly

uncomfortable being treated with kindness when he had been hostile toward her son since his arrival.

"He's on the computer in his room. Zach, you've got a visitor!"

Logan stood awkwardly on the doorstep, wishing he could simply walk away. However concern for Laina kept his feet firmly planted where they were.

"I'm running late for work so I hope you'll excuse me. Zach!"

A faint reply came from the other end of the house. "Coming Mom!"

"Go on through to the kitchen." Caroline beamed in her friendly manner. "I'm leaving now, Zach. I'll be home around eleven tonight."

"Okay." Zach's voice sounded closer.

Caroline brushed past Logan and headed for the station wagon parked in the driveway. Zach entered the hallway and stopped in his tracks when he recognized the visitor standing in the front entrance.

"What do you want?"

Logan wondered at her unusual hours. "Where does your mom work?"

"She's a nurse at Walkerville Hospital. Why are you here?" Zach crossed his arms and leaned against the kitchen door frame, staring at Logan across the short hallway. A smile tugged at his lips, evidence of spiteful enjoyment over the obvious discomfort Logan was feeling as he stood just inside the entrance, aware that his presence was unwelcome.

"Laina's in trouble and I need your help to find her. She hasn't shown up at work for the last two days and she's not at her house. I don't know where else to look." Logan cast aside the last remnant of his pride. "I was hoping you might know where she hangs out."

Zach pushed away from the door frame and un-crossed his arms, his demeanor instantly changing. "What happened?"

"I'll let her tell you that. First we have to find her."

"I think I know where she'll be." Zach followed him onto the front porch.

Logan closed the door while Zach pulled on his runners. Together they headed for the woods behind Zach's house.

~

"I think someone's onto us," the technician spoke softly into his mobile phone as he drove along the dirt track on his way home after a busy day.

There was no one to hear him out in this vast wil-derness, however his nervousness over the whole affair was rapidly becoming paranoia.

"How do you know?" The businessman sounded

unhappy at the prospect of losing the lucrative deal.

"Some people have been sniffing around." The computer whizz kept his eyes on the road ahead of him.

"You are paranoid. No one could possibly know what we are planning."

"All the same, I'd feel a whole lot better if we moved the date of exchange forward."

There was silence as the shady character considered the suggestion. To lose this unprecedented opportunity was unthinkable. Too much was at stake, and the technician knew it.

"That may be wise. Have the data and designs ready by next week. I will call you to confirm a time to meet and I will have the money. Make sure you have the merchandise." The businessman's cool insistence was intimidating.

The computer mastermind was beginning to have second thoughts. What would happen if he backed out? Knowing the desperation that existed around the world for this kind of technology, those he was dealing with would consider his life a minimal price to pay to own it. Bearing that thought in mind, he mentally planned the last few steps he needed to take in order to complete this deal.

~

Laina stared into her wooden food box in the tree house and sighed. She needed to go shopping. She had the money, just not the inclination to set foot anywhere Rylan might find her.

She frowned over the mind-set she had fallen into the last couple of days. She was living in fear.

This has to stop.

Although she was unsure of how to go about it.

I need your help, Lord. I can't live my life cloistered away like a hermit, afraid to set foot outside these woods. But if I do come forward about Rylan, I'm afraid of what might happen.

Afraid. Laina pondered that word. Either direction she considered taking held a great amount of uncertainty. Maybe she just had to stand up and step out despite her fear?

She was still debating what to do when two masculine voices floated on the late afternoon breeze, drifting through the open tree house door. She was instantly alert.

Laina peered through the window, however leaves fluttering on the branches outside restricted visibility. She went to the doorway and peaked outside. Two familiar forms strode into the clearing below. Laina relaxed and sat on the edge of the platform, legs dangling over.

She could not resist a quip. "What brings you to my neck of the woods?"

"Very funny," Zach replied dryly. "Here I was worried sick that something was wrong and you're up there making jokes."

Both he and Logan stood at the base of the tree, craning their necks to look up. Laina sobered. Maybe it was time the truth came out?

"I'm glad you came." She swung onto the rope ladder and began her descent. "I have something I need to tell you. Well, two things actually."

A glimpse over her shoulder caught Zach and Logan exchanging curious glances. Laina dropped the last few feet to the ground and turned to face them. The second she did, Zach's gaze landed upon the dark hand and finger shaped bruises on her neck. His eyes flew to meet hers, carrying with them a thousand questions, and a new flame of anger.

"Who did this to you?"

"That's part of what I need to tell you. Wil and Nick will need to know as well. Come and sit down." She indicated her favorite grassy patch beside the creek.

Logan and Zach complied, both clearly wanting answers. Laina sat with them and began to tell her story.

"You both know my dad died in a car accident when I was thirteen and I came to live with Uncle

Rylan. Dad never had much to do with him and it wasn't until I moved into his home that I understood why.

"Everyone is charmed by his amiable manner but when he's behind closed doors he's a different man. He's verbally nasty and cold. When he drinks, he becomes physically abusive. It became clear to me after only a week that he never wanted to become my guardian, but for some reason he agreed. A year ago I decided I'd had enough of being his doormat and I moved out."

Both boys exchanged surprised glances.

"But I thought that you..." Logan tried to organize perplexed thoughts. "The whole town believes you still live with..."

Laina studied her friends pragmatically. "At first I came and went as I had need. Then I started working for Gracie and I went home less and less. I visited for a signature on a permission slip here, an official form there..." Laina shrugged. "For a long time now I've been living by myself and paying my own way."

A horrified expression came over Zach's face and Logan looked troubled. Laina hurried to reassure them.

"I have a good life. It's peaceful."

Zach was aghast. "Don't tell me you live in this tree house?"

"I've never sought anyone's pity and I'm not seeking it now. I'm telling you because you're my friends and you have a right to know, especially since it now involves you. I've discovered that Uncle Rylan is involved in the H5-40 project."

"What?" Logan exclaimed in disbelief.

"How do you know?" Zach chimed in at the same time.

Laina took a deep breath and calmly explained her interaction with her uncle two days prior.

Zach was the first to respond. "You've got to report him!"

"This gives us the evidence we need to convince Dan Fisher and Sheriff Hawkins," Logan interjected.

"Is that all you can think about? Proving our case? Laina's uncle just choked and threatened her and still all you care about is H5-40!"

Logan turned on Zach angrily. "I care about her, city boy. If we prove the case about H5-40, they'll take us seriously and do something about Rylan Jackson."

Zach opened his mouth to argue and Laina held up her hands. "Hold it you two! Before you come to blows, you should know I think you're both right."

They passed each other a hostile glance before giving Laina their attention.

"I just realized before you got here that I've been living in fear for the last two days. I want to be free of my uncle for good. I'm just not sure how to go about it. I don't want to end up in the welfare system and I don't want Uncle Rylan finding out I reported him. His reaction will be even worse when he discovers I destroyed his reputation."

Logan seethed. "If he so much as lays a hand on you I'll-"

"Yeah I know," Laina cut him off, "you'll wipe the floor with him."

"And that's after I've given him a taste of his own medicine," Zach added his two pence worth.

Laina sighed wearily. She was struggling with her own fair share of anger and resentment toward her uncle, which she knew God did not want her to harbor. She had to set an example of Christ's love in this situation, or it might spiral out of control.

Please God, help me to love Uncle Rylan in what I say and do? I choose to forgive him. But having done that, does it mean I let his abuse continue unchecked? Laina had no answer. She only knew she had to come forward with the truth and leave the outcome in God's hands.

"Guys, I need you to take a walk with me into town."

~

"And you say Rylan did this?" Sheriff Hawkins clarified, struggling with the evidence before him and the man he trusted.

"Yes," Laina answered matter-of-factly.

"What made him so angry?" The sheriff closely surveyed the bruises on Laina's arm and neck, finally stepping back to listen to her story.

"I asked him a question."

"And what was that?" Dan Fisher was leaning against the side of his desk, his eyes shining with disbelief and a good measure of shock.

"I asked him if he was involved in the H5-40 project." Laina studied the two men before her and watched as the full import of her statement sank in.

They were standing in the Icy Creek Sheriff's Office. Logan and Zach waited on the other side of the counter, present for moral support. Sheriff Hawkins' expression was grave and he glanced at Deputy Fisher, raising one enquiring eyebrow. Finally he turned to Laina.

"I'd like to have your permission to take a picture of those bruises for evidence." His solemn gaze then encompassed Zach and Logan as well. "Then I need all of you to tell me again about this H5-40 thing from the very beginning."

10

"What do you suppose they'll do?" Zach wondered aloud as he, Logan and Laina wandered down the main street.

"He said he would be in touch with the welfare department and that he would also have a talk with Mr. Jackson," Logan recounted part of the earlier conversation.

"Do you suppose they'll check out the factory?" Laina queried.

Logan stuffed his hands in his pockets. "I hope so. Either way I still think we should go Friday, just for a look."

Laina was still unsure of that plan.

"Let's tell Nick and Wil the news," Zach suggested.

Laina brightened. "Hey, I've got an idea. You guys bring them to the tree house and I'll cook you all dinner."

Logan raised a skeptical brow. "How are you going to do that? You've got no stove."

"I have my ways. Just be at my place by six and I'll

have it ready."

Zach grinned. "She's a good cook, trust me."

Logan did not appear thrilled that Zach had enjoyed the pleasure of Laina's cooking. If Laina didn't know better, she would say he was suffering from a twinge of jealousy.

"I'll round up the boys," he volunteered unenthusiastically.

"I'll give Laina a hand."

"No," Logan objected a little too hastily. "You fetch Nick and I'll get Wil. It'll be quicker that way."

Zach shrugged, completely oblivious to the fact Logan was keeping him from being alone with her. Laina was a little surprised at his unprecedented possessive streak.

"Okay. Will you be alright?" Zach double checked with her.

"Yep." She was already plotting the menu. She would stop by the store and buy some rice and a few other spicy ingredients to make a tasty Spanish dish. All she would need was one pot over a campfire and half an hour to cook it. "I'll meet you there."

They parted ways. As Laina headed for the general store she reflected. It had been a difficult day and yet a rewarding one. Tonight she would have dinner guests at her wilderness home for the very first time.

"Tomorrow morning at seven it is," Nick confirmed.

Wil nodded agreement and polished off his last mouthful of Spanish rice. The group of five was just finishing off the delicious meal Laina had whipped up over her campfire. She had shared the truth about her uncle and between them all, they had gained a fuller picture of the issues surrounding H5-40.

They had collectively decided to ride their bikes to the factory, intending to take a camera this time for evidence. Although still a little unsure about checking out the premises when Rylan was so against her being anywhere in that vicinity, Laina had agreed to go along. They did not intend to trespass, rather to simply get a closer look and maybe even a picture to prove it existed.

"How do you do it?" Nick inquired amicably as he sat his empty paper plate aside on the grass below the tree house.

Laina was puzzled. "How do I do what?"

"Live out here, cook, wash, stay warm, store your food, that kind of stuff."

The others listened attentively, also looking curious over how she had managed to survive and make a life for herself with so little.

"Life is fairly basic, I'll admit, but it's quiet and

it's peaceful. When cooking, I either buy canned or packet food that can be stored, or I buy it fresh to make each night over a fire. As for storage, how do you think people got along before refrigerators were invented?" she challenged with a grin.

Zach shrugged and the others looked clueless. Wil was the only one brave enough to venture an answer.

"An ice box?"

Laina smiled. "You bet! I've got a hole dug on the other side of the oak with an ice box that I cover over. The cold earth keeps the ice longer and I only have to replace it once or twice a week. Plus, it keeps the critters out."

Nick's eyes were inquisitive. "How do you get along without a washing machine or running water?"

Laina chuckled. "Are you joking? I've got fresh water running right past my front door every day. It's good for washing, drinking and reeling in a tasty fish every now and then."

Nick raised surprised brows. Laina smiled in amusement as she tried to imagine how Zach would cope without electricity and modern technology. Logan's usually guarded expression held admiration. She guessed he would trade his responsibilities for her carefree existence in a heartbeat.

Wil's face reflected sadness. She knew he had a secure, loving family and a nice home. She looked away from those intuitive eyes lest he see how much she longed for what he had. To be honest, she didn't like having to endure the harshness of winter snows in her draughty tree house without proper insulation. However, she had learnt to be content.

"I don't know why you all think it's such a big deal. It's not much different from the way our pioneer ancestors lived."

"Yeah well, some of us have grown accustomed to the comforts of a house with electricity and indoor plumbing," Nick admitted.

"You're a bunch of girls if you ask me," Laina teased cheekily.

"Is that the truth?" Zach's eyes took on a mischievous gleam.

Before Laina knew what was happening, he had sprung to his feet and hoisted her over his shoulder, fireman style. She shrieked and laughed as he carted her toward the creek and with one thrust, tossed her in the water. The evening was hot and the water was refreshingly cool, yet the temperature shock still caused her to surface gasping for breath.

He laughed outright at her 'drowned cat' look. "Are you enjoying your evening bath?"

She wiped wet hair away from her face and stared at him in astonishment. An arm around his torso and a sudden crash from behind sent Zach toppling into the creek. Laughter and cheers arose from Logan and Wil who had witnessed Nick's playful tackle. The next thing they knew, Wil leapt into the fray and a water fight ensued.

"Come on Logan!" Nick cajoled. "It's beautiful in here!"

"No thanks." Logan seemed unable to let go his reserve and join his friends.

"He's just afraid I'll drown his sorry case," Zach baited with a teasing grin.

Logan's gaze narrowed and he strode to the creek bank, hands on his hips and his expression looking suspiciously like he might take up the challenge. Without warning, he jumped in shoes and all, and took Zach under with him.

Laughter and shrieks of playful enjoyment lifted heavenward, along with the stout branches bearing rich green foliage surrounding the creek. They stretched into the darkening expanse above, which winked gleefully with the first appearance of glittering evening stars.

11

"Go faster, city boy, or is that the best you can do?"

Logan sailed past Zach on his mountain bike, the tires kicking up dust and stones.

Zach laughed mischievously and grinned. He pedaled harder and edged ahead of him.

"Would you guys please slow down?" Laina called as she struggled to keep up with their maniacal pace.

"Yeah, take it easy you two!" Nick shouted, looking more than a little annoyed over their rivalry.

The five teenagers were riding their bikes along the deserted logging track further and further into the wilderness. Laina guessed that they had been pedaling for three hours or more and the intense sun was steadily creeping toward its peak in the glaringly blue summer sky.

"It's ninety degrees Fahrenheit!" Wil added his objection. "You'll get heat stroke."

"Boys!" Laina harrumphed. "Ridiculously competitive and hopeless show offs."

"Thanks Laina," Nick remarked dryly with a grin.

He was a couple of yards in front and Wil was abreast of her. They were riding at a comfortable, sustainable rate.

Laina could not resist a giggle. "Sorry guys, you two are the exception."

"You're all heart," Wil remarked.

Laina was amazed at the transformation that had come over him since the previous evening. He seemed to have relaxed around her and Zach, talking and laughing as freely as he did with Nick and Logan. It was a pleasure to see the real Wil Genner.

Zach and Logan raced ahead up the next hill and around a bend out of sight. Laina rolled her eyes and Wil just shook his head.

"How much further do you think it is to the factory?" Nick wondered aloud.

"We can stop and have a look at the map and my compass."

"Alright." Nick braked.

Laina came to a slow stop and dismounted. She flicked the stand down on her bike and moved closer to Wil who was unfolding a map and taking his compass from his pocket. Nick carefully laid his bike on the track and wandered over. All three were hot and sweaty. They bent their heads over the map while Wil triangulated their position.

"We're here." He pointed to a specific section of

road on the chart. "And I'm estimating that the factory is roughly there."

"So how far have we got to go?" Laina was mystified when it came to the mathematics involved in
navigation. She preferred landmarks and memory to
maps and compasses. Yet in this circumstance, she
was grateful that Wil knew how to use both.

"It's about five more miles." He folded the map
away again.

"That'll only take another fifteen minutes," Nick
estimated.

"Less, if you're as hot-headed as those two goofs
tearing down the road." Laina indicated the track
ahead.

Nick laughed and they got back on their bikes and
started off down the road. They rode in companionable silence for another ten minutes.

Lining the track were tall pines with thick trunks.
Their size was a rough indication of their age. Laina
wondered what they would say if they could talk.
How many travelers had passed by them over the
years? What secrets were hidden within their silent
ranks? Could they help unravel this latest mystery
if they were able to talk? They stood there tall and
proud, the occasional branch creaking with movement and their needles whispering with the gentle
breeze.

Laina's gaze drifted idly over the tranquil scenery surrounding her. Her heart nearly leapt out of her chest when two figures suddenly bolted from the trees, straight into their path. Nick exclaimed in surprise and all three braked hard to avoid collision. It took only a moment before recognition calmed Laina's nerves.

Zach's dark brown eyes sparkled with merriment as he and Logan stood proud as punch in the center of the track. Logan was grinning mischievously, obviously enjoying the fact that he and Zach had nearly scared the wits out of their buddies.

"Are you two out of your minds?" Nick growled as the adrenalin pumping through his veins began to abate.

"You scared us half to death!" Laina added her protest.

Logan smiled broadly. "Getting a little jumpy?"

"Considering what happened to us the last time we were out here, yeah, I guess you could say I'm a little jumpy." She glared at him in annoyance.

"It can't be far to the factory now," Wil broke into their minor squabble. His expression was displeased and his voice subdued. Yet he refrained from comment to avoid exacerbating the argument. "We should hide our bikes in the trees and walk the rest of the way."

123

What if they had managed to fix the machine in the last three days? Laina shuddered at the thought.

"Good thinking Wil." Nick cast a disgruntled look Logan and Zach's way.

Laina, Nick and Wil leant their bikes against a tree out of sight. Logan and Zach followed them.

"I think we should walk the rest of the way under the cover of these trees," Laina commented.

"I think so too," Logan agreed.

Wil consulted his map and pointed south. "It's that way."

The group silently set off in that direction. From here on they were flirting with danger.

~

Rylan walked down the sterile white corridor, passing another computer lab, the staff lounge and several offices. His alert eyes briefly scanned the staff room as he passed the doorway. Dirk wasn't there.

Sweat gathered in small glistening beads on Rylan's forehead from nervous tension. He had to get his hands on the software. How could he do it without being caught? If that nerd would only leave the lab for a lunch break like everyone else!

The workaholic never seemed to tire of tinkering with his computer and the projects under construction. There was no doubt that Dirk Wyler was a genius. But as to his loyalties, Rylan had doubts. Serious doubts.

Rylan continued down the corridor to the main lab. He peered around the door frame into the sterile room. Sure enough, Dirk was at his desk, fingers madly tapping away at his keyboard. His desk consisted of a long counter against the far stark white wall. The surface was strewn with the hawk's parts; microchips, wires, circuit boards and the outer casings that contained heat sensors.

Since the incident several days ago, Dirk and Dr. Jefferson had assumed the massive task of dismantling and repairing the machine. It seemed to consume every waking hour. Yet even passionate inventor, Dr. Albert Jefferson, took a lunch break.

Rylan wondered how he could possibly distract the younger man long enough to gain access to his computer. He was pondering his next move when nature solved the problem.

Dirk's stool scraped against the floor and his footsteps echoed in the otherwise silent room. Rylan quickly turned and strolled in the direction he had come, hoping to appear as though he had simply passed by. Dirk's steps retreated in the opposite direction down the corridor toward the men's room. Rylan heard the bathroom door open and close.

He quickly doubled back and hastened to Dirk's desk. The usually paranoid technician had left his computer unlocked. Rylan supposed the geek figured he would be gone only a matter of minutes. He didn't have long.

Rylan drew up the file he wanted, the digital blueprints for H5-40. He inserted a miniature disc into the disc drive and transferred the file. A bead of sweat trickled down the side of his face. He wiped it away with his crisp white coat sleeve. The downloading seemed to take forever. In actuality it was only a minute or two.

Then Rylan did the unthinkable. He removed his disc containing the plans and programming for the hawk and then inserted another, this one containing a virus. He uploaded it and hastily removed the disc, slipping both into his pants pocket. He glanced over his shoulder. He only had seconds before Dirk would re-emerge from the bathroom.

Rylan exited the blueprint file, leaving the screen as he had found it, and planted a listening bug under the desk. He then left the room. He was greatly relieved to find the corridor still empty.

He hurried up the passageway and ducked into the staff lounge, pasting on a charming smile and greeting his colleagues with easy familiarity. He needed an alibi for when Dirk's computer suddenly crashed, which would be when he tried to open another program. The virus would begin its devastating work by completely wiping the memory of the entire network within the facility.

Rylan was secretly pleased with his cunningly devised plan. It had taken a while to complete. Siphoning off the entire facilities' files and programs to be able to restore them all later, had been time consuming. They were stored away in a security deposit box on several external hard drives. He smiled. In minutes he would be the only person with a copy of the revolutionary software.

~

"Wow, would you look at that!" Zach exclaimed in a whisper filled with awe.

All five teenagers stared in wonder at the enormous facility looking completely out of place in the middle of dense forest. This was no factory. The modern structure was one story high, which made it difficult to see due to the towering pines on all sides. The building was made of large white cement panels, interrupted only by slim windows stretching from ceiling to floor. Above two large glass doors at the entrance was a sign that read 'Astro Enterprises'. Surrounding the premises was a tall wire fence, and if

Laina's hearing could be trusted, it was electrified.

Her gaze followed the line of the fence to her right. From her position crouched behind a thick spruce beside Zach, she spotted what appeared to be the main gate. Posted at the entrance was a white booth with glass windows. Inside Laina could see the outline of a guard.

"Are you getting all of this?" Logan asked Zach, who had brought along his digital video camera.

"You bet!" Zach grinned and panned across the building and its compound.

Suddenly an alarm went off. The five teens watched in surprise and then horror as armed men poured from the glass doors.

"How did they detect us?" Nick asked in bewilderment.

"I don't know but I'm not staying around to find out." Logan took off in the direction they had come.

Wil and Nick were right behind him. Zach filmed the guards shouting orders as they ran across the compound to the main gate.

"We don't have enough time," he stated to Laina who was crouched beside him, reluctant to leave him behind.

In seconds they would all be overrun and the evidence they had captured on camera would no doubt be destroyed. He removed the memory card from the camera and took a spare from his pocket, slotting it into place. Then he slipped the one containing the footage into his sock. If they were searched, no one would look there. He hoped.

"Zach, we have to go!" Laina hissed, watching as five armed men split up at the gate.

Two disappeared into the woods on the other side of the road, while three began to stalk warily through the trees near where Zach and Laina were hiding. They were wearing plain black cotton trousers and black shirts and caps, each bearing a business logo. In their hands they toted fully loaded automatic rifles, the type of stuff Laina had only ever seen in movies. She was terrified!

Zach picked up a nearby stick the thickness of his arm. Laina read his intent and balked. If he tried to defend himself against the men now stealthily creeping toward them, he would be shot.

"Zach, no!" she whispered furiously.

He glared at her crossly for several seconds, his eyes warning her to keep quiet. Laina was scared out of her wits, but she would not let Zach get himself killed while he tried to be heroic. She stepped from behind the spruce with her hands raised.

"Don't shoot!"

Her eyes widened in fright when the closest guard, only five paces away, spun in her direction with his rifle barrel aimed at her chest.

"It's a bunch of kids!" he called over his shoulder to his comrades, his weapon still trained on her.

Now standing in the open, Laina could see the other two men skulking between the trees twenty to thirty yards away. They had fanned out and were listening intently and studying the soil, crushed by three pairs of running feet.

"Come out from behind the tree!" the man nearest her demanded in a booming voice that Zach did not dare argue with.

He obeyed, casting Laina a betrayed glare.

"Drop the stick!" The guard's eyes snapped with tension.

Zach hesitated for several seconds. Laina glanced sideways to see what was taking him so long. She was infuriated to see a rebellious glint in his eyes.

"This is not a game, Zach. Do as the man says!"

Zach reluctantly tossed the stick aside, passing her an angry glance.

"Alright," the guard continued, satisfied the boy had complied, "on your faces with your hands behind your backs."

"You've watched way too many action movies!" Zach complained even as he and Laina did as they were told.

"This ain't no movie kid," the man replied with a

hint of humor in his voice. "You're trespassing on private property and so are your friends."

"What friends?" Zach tried to mislead him.

The guard smiled in knowing amusement as he approached them. "The ones that tripped our sensors. There's five of you."

Zach raised surprised brows and glanced sideways at Laina, who was also on her belly in the dirt. "What sensors?"

The guard shouldered his weapon and cuffed them both. "You're beginning to bother me, kid. You'd do well to keep your trap shut for a while."

Laina nodded toward the man frisking Zach. "I agree with him."

The boy in question rolled his eyes in annoyance. He was then yanked to his feet.

"Alright, get up."

Laina instantly obeyed.

"Walk ahead of us to the gate over yonder and don't try anything."

"You're telling me not to try anything?" Laina was incredulous. Her heart rate rocketed as the situation spiraled out of control. "I'm not the one holding a gun. I hope you haven't got an itchy trigger finger mister."

12

Laina and Zach were thrust into a windowless room with plain white walls and a white tiled floor. There was no furniture, not even a chair. The door slammed shut behind them and they both heard a clicking sound, which Laina guessed to be a key turning in the dead bolt on the other side. They exchanged grave glances.

"I'm beginning to regret listening to Logan," Zach remarked with relative calm.

"I wish I'd gone with my gut instinct and spent the day fishing."

Laina let her eyes roam the sparse room from ceiling to floor. Inwardly she was praying. *I'm sorry I came, Lord. I should have realized that gut feeling was actually You warning me.*

Peace. The foreign thought impressed itself upon her mind. *Be anxious for nothing.*

Is that you, Lord Jesus? Laina questioned the soothing voice speaking to her spirit.

Be at peace. It came again, gentle and reassuring. *I*

am in control.

Laina exhaled in relief and her heart was suddenly calm. She leaned against a wall and slid down until she was sitting on the floor. All she could do now was wait and see what would happen next.

~

"What? No!" Dirk shrieked in disbelief and stared at his computer screen which displayed the words 'no signal'. "This can't be happening!"

He had merely tried to open the file he had been working on when a pop up box indicated that everything on his computer was being deleted. He rebooted the machine and waited impatiently for the desktop image to show up. However when it did, no program icons were visible.

He hurriedly attempted to access the design software used to open plans of the model for H5-40. Nothing. No program and no files.

"Oh you have got to be kidding!" Dismayed, he typed in a frenzy to access the backup server. Nothing. Not even a word processing file remained. Dirk ran distressed fingers through his closely cropped brown hair and ran for the staff lounge.

"Al! It's gone, all of it's gone!"

Albert Jefferson was sitting comfortably on a couch

in the corner of the room, chatting amiably with Rylan Jackson. The alarm that had sounded only minutes before had cleared the room of most of its occupants. The majority of them were curious about the intruders and had gone to see what the ruckus was about. Only a few unruffled souls remained behind, unwilling to allow their lunch break to be interrupted by yet another false alarm. Rylan and Albert were two of those unperturbed individuals. Both looked up in surprise when Dirk burst through the doorway shouting.

"What's gone?" Albert's brow furrowed in puzzlement over the pure panic exuding from every pore of Dirk's body.

"The software, the files, the blueprints and programs, it's all gone! A virus has just wiped our entire network. Even the backups are gone."

Albert and Rylan exchanged worried glances. Dirk spun and headed back toward the lab at a run.

~

Roughly thirty minutes of anxious waiting had passed while Zach paced the room trying to figure a way out of this mess. He had somehow stepped through his cuffed hands so that they were now in front of him. Laina watched him do another circle of the room and test the doorknob for the umpteenth time.

It occurred to her then that Zach's trust was in himself and that was why he was so restless all the time. Because he refused to let God into his life, he had no one but himself to rely on in troubled times. That explained his more aggressive nature.

"You know, I used to be like you" Laina commented thoughtfully.

"How's that?" Zach stopped pacing long enough to look at her quizzically.

"I used to be driven by fear and the need to survive, although I didn't strike out at others the way you do when you feel threatened."

"What are you on about?" Zach's attention was now fully on her and he looked none too happy.

"You're angry at God for what He allowed when you let Him take charge of your life. As a result you've pushed Him away and now you're trying to control it yourself, only it's not working. You're angry, scared, empty and restless."

"Just shut up Laina!" Zach slashed the air with his cuffed hands.

His angry eyes betrayed him. They told her she had been one hundred percent accurate.

"What do you know about me?"

"I used to be where you are," Laina replied with

compassion.

"But now you've got it all figured out, haven't you?" he retorted sarcastically.

Laina shook her head in irritation and looked away. Why wouldn't he face the truth? "I don't think I'm better than you, if that's what you're getting at." She made eye contact. "I only brought it up because I can see you're so unhappy and I know if you'll go to Jesus He'll give you peace. Then you won't have to carry the burden that comes with running your own life."

"My life is just fine the way it is."

Laina calmly held his irate gaze. "Then sit down and relax. Prove to me that your way works better than mine. Show me that trusting yourself gives you peace and maybe I'll be convinced."

Zach howled with frustration and turned away from her. Laina could not resist an amused smile. She was right and he knew it.

Suddenly the lock released and the door burst open. It crashed against the wall. Three more teenagers were thrust inside. Logan landed on his stomach on the floor, his hands cuffed behind his back. Wil managed to stay on his feet while Nick lost his balance and ended up on his knees. The door slammed shut behind them.

Nick struggled to his feet. "Something's going on out there."

"You mean other than security going nuts because of us?" Zach answered dryly.

Wil sank to the floor beside Laina. "Yeah."

"What is it?" Laina glanced at him inquisitively.

"I heard some people talking while those goons shoved us down the corridor. Something about a virus wiping all of their computers."

Zach raised curious eyebrows. "Let's just hope they don't blame us."

"None of us have the skill to do something like that," Nick remarked.

Zach grinned. "Speak for yourself."

Logan smiled and Nick and Wil looked at each other and shrugged. The group settled in, left once again to wait and wonder.

~

Rylan spent the better part of the next hour pretending to be just as panicked as everyone else in the building, madly scrambling to rescue files that were irretrievable.

"Rylan," Eric's voice broke into his thoughts.

Rylan glanced up from the computer on his desk in his small office. He was one of the few lucky technicians that not only had his own office, but one with a large glass window that looked out over vast forest.

"Yes boss?" He waited expectantly for the well dressed, rotund man to speak.

"I'd like you to check the backgrounds of the five kids we caught trespassing today. I've just sent Austin to interrogate them but as you know, he can get a little intense."

"Austin Keffler?"

"Yes."

"Sir, intense isn't quite the way I would describe him."

"Then maybe I'm a little more gracious than you, Jackson." Eric smiled broadly with twinkling eyes. "But he is good at his job."

"Which is what exactly?" Rylan's mind conjured up a memory of the curly haired, dark eyed man with the quick temper.

"Management and containment of delicate situations."

In other words, he's a CIA thug here to keep things under wraps, Rylan thought but did not say. "Sure boss, you know I'm always willing to lend a helping hand."

"You're a good man to have around, Jackson."

"Thank you sir." Rylan nodded and his boss left the room.

The system crash had caused him to forget they had some visitors. He had a sneaking feeling he knew exactly who they were. He decided that it might be best to delegate this task to someone those nosy teenagers did not know.

~

"Who are you and why were you snooping around the perimeter?" Austin Keffler demanded.

His cold gaze sent chills down Laina's spine.

"We were only curious. We wanted to know what that thing was that gassed Laina, Zach and Logan," Nick explained honestly.

The five friends were lined up sitting against the far wall, as the forbidding man standing before them had gruffly instructed. He narrowed his shrewd gaze.

He pointed at Nick and Wil. "You two were there?"

Wil looked scared stiff. "Up a tree sir."

The light of understanding entered the man's eyes. "So it was you who threw pine cones at our machine?"

"It was that or be gassed and fall out of the tree and die. It's us who should be mad at you!" Nick defended. "We were in a national park and your stupid contraption nearly killed us!"

"Yeah, that makes you liable," Zach interjected.

"I'd say it makes us even considering you broke it."

"I've got a hunch the court might see it differently,"

Logan countered. "Since your actions put our lives in jeopardy."

"And you were testing a dangerous machine on public property," Nick added.

Austin sighed and judging by the clenching of his fists, he was restraining the urge to hit someone or something. This was going nowhere fast. He quietly regarded them, seemingly weighing his options. By the dark malevolent glint in his eyes, Laina guessed none of them were good. She understood he needed their silence. The question was how he planned to go about it. Blackmail? Bribery? By legal means? The look in his eyes suggested he would prefer a more permanent method.

Just then the door opened and an older gentleman quietly slipped inside. His intelligent eyes assessed the five intruders and softened when they rested upon Wil. Fear and uncertainty played across the young man's face. Laina saw that the other boys were hiding their trepidation through aggression as they argued with Austin.

"Mr. Keffler, if I may?" He stepped forward and indicated his desire to speak to the teens with a sweep of his hand and a gentlemanly nod of his head.

"They're all yours, Albert." Austin's relief was immediate and he gladly left the room. The door closed behind him with a resounding thud against the frame.

"Well, it would seem that you have managed to make Mr. Keffler extremely frustrated." Albert smiled in amusement. "Which is quite easy to do on the best of days, I will admit."

Wil's uncertain expression turned to one of hope, while Zach and Logan regarded the older man with distrust. Nick seemed to relax somewhat and Laina could not resist a smile.

"We weren't trespassing," Zach defended. "If we'd tried to get through that fence then yeah, I can understand the guards going nuts. But we were just curiously looking in. We didn't touch a thing and we weren't *going* to."

"I understand that." The scientist crouched down in front of them at eye level.

Nick was bewildered. "Then why all of the commotion?"

"Well gentleman, and young lady," he added and nodded respectfully to Laina, "we are working on some top secret projects for the government."

"H5-40?" Laina guessed.

Albert smiled indulgently. "I can see you are all very astute. Yes, projects like H5-40. Projects that can help our soldiers in times of war. Projects that can save lives."

"That machine you call the hawk nearly killed us!"

Logan snapped, evidently unwilling to buy the placating speech they were being fed.

"I'm very sorry about that. I realize now it was a mistake to test it in such circumstances and I'm sorry for what you went through. But surely you can understand the importance of our country owning this kind of technology."

"I guess," Nick admitted.

"You're not buying this rubbish are you?" Logan looked jaded and cynical.

"He's making sense," Nick leaned around Zach to argue.

Albert's eyes twinkled with merriment. He clearly enjoyed young people and their brutal honesty.

"Now I want you to imagine something for me."

All five sets of eyes regarded Albert with a different emotion: Zach with shrewdness, Logan with suspicion, Nick with curiosity, Wil with openness and Laina with interest.

"Imagine hostile nations or terrorist organizations getting their hands on the hawk. Our soldiers would stand no chance in battle. The enemy would know their every move and would wipe them out without hesitation." The gentleman paused, allowing time to consider this scary prospect.

Laina silently conceded that he had a point.

"Then turn the paradigm around. Imagine what

142

our soldiers could do in the fight against terror, for example, with a piece of equipment like H5-40. They would be able to infiltrate the most difficult terrain that has up till now, prevented the capture of terrorist masterminds, or has come at a great cost to American lives. They can take out terrorists hiding in mosques and schools and amongst the innocent public, without harming civilians. Can you see why it's important that what we are doing here remains a secret? How the guards responded may seem like an overreaction, but think what would happen if someone untrustworthy were to get their hands on this project."

Logan was outraged. "Oh come on! We're just a bunch of kids poking around and they threatened us with automatic weapons!"

"We *were* kind of suspicious, you gotta admit that." Zach was beginning to side with Nick.

Logan's eyes narrowed, a clear indication that he would not be swayed.

"You're going to ask us to keep this quiet, aren't you?" Nick predicted.

Albert smiled and shrugged helplessly. "Unfortunately, yes."

Laina shared Logan's misgivings to a certain degree. "Can you guarantee you won't be doing any more testing where people could get hurt?"

"Yes. The company does not want to be liable anymore than you or I want someone to be harmed," the scientist replied with gravity. "That incident earlier this week was a rather large wake-up call for everyone here."

"You know what mister, I believe you're telling us the truth," Zach observed discerningly.

"Gullible," Logan muttered under his breath.

"No, I believe he's telling the truth too," Laina chipped in.

"Then you're both gullible." Logan eyed them testily.

Nick once again leaned around Zach to speak to Logan. "I believe him as well. What do you think Wil?"

Wil stared at the older man for several silent seconds, reading him carefully. "He's a good egg. The other guy was rotten, but this one is telling the truth."

Logan snorted in disagreement but said nothing.

"So, what happens now?"

Albert nodded thoughtfully. "I'll make a deal with you."

"What's that?" Zach was suddenly wary.

"I'll let you all off the hook and will even give you a ride back to town if you will agree to keep H5-40 and our work here a secret."

Nick opened his mouth to object.

"And I promise you that there will be no more test-ing in places where it is likely there will be people."

Each of the five faces before Albert were thought-ful. Logan did not look happy about the deal, yet Laina supposed he would agree to just about any-thing to get out of here.

Nick shrugged. "I'm in." He looked at his friends one by one to see what their decision would be.

"I guess it's okay," Laina agreed slowly.

"You're not doing anything illegal up here are you?" Zach asked suspiciously.

Albert chuckled. "No. I assure you everything we are doing is completely by the book."

"But you're a private enterprise on government property," Zach pointed out.

"We have a sanction to research and develop here, provided that we only sell our products to the U.S. government."

Zach raised thoughtful brows and then shrugged.

"So it's cool for us to go hiking and fishing out here still?" Nick checked with the man.

"Yes." Albert smiled broadly. "We will be testing our equipment elsewhere from now on."

Wil sighed with relief and smiled at Laina who grinned in return.

"If that's the case," Logan interjected, "then can you tell those trigger happy commandos to lay off if we bump into them again?"

"Do I have your word you won't come sneaking around our lab anymore?" Albert asked him directly.

A half smile tugged at Logan's lips. "Sure."

Albert eyed him doubtfully and Logan's smile broadened.

"Really, I mean it. No more snooping."

"Yeah, you've answered our questions about what's going on out here. That's all we wanted to know," Nick reassured him.

Albert's next smile was warm and relaxed. "Good. We have a deal. Now, if you will all kindly wait here, I shall see about obtaining your release."

"Sure thing. We ain't goin' nowhere," Logan replied dryly, causing the scientist to chuckle on his way out.

13

"How do you think the virus got into the system?" Austin asked Dirk minutes after he left the meddling teenagers to sweat it out in the isolation room.

They were alone in the lab in front of Dirk's computer.

"I can't be sure. It could have been uploaded onto the network from any computer in the facility."

"And you don't think it got into the system when someone accessed the internet?"

"No. Our firewall is too strong for us to be hacked. We've got more protection than most government agencies do. Whoever did this was from the inside."

"Sabotage? Who would want to do that?"

Dirk continued to tap away madly at his keyboard, doing his best to rid the system of the virus. "My guess is that someone is onto us and wanted to prevent the software from being stolen."

Austin narrowed his gaze suspiciously. That was a reasonable assumption. "Albert Jefferson?"

"Al? Not a chance. He's too trusting to ever think

someone from here would steal his designs."

Austin was puzzled. "If not Albert then who?"

Dirk abruptly stopped typing and turned slowly around on his swiveling stool. His eyes were wide with realization. "Rylan Jackson. He's the only other person here with the ability to create a virus that could circumnavigate our antivirus protection. I forgot he used to design antivirus software at his previous company. He once told me he used to invent viruses to test the programs he put together, and I saw him walking past the lab on my way to the bathroom. He was the only person around at the time."

"A lot of people walk by your lab, Dirk. It's on the way to the staff lounge, which is where Jackson was when everything crashed."

"Yes, but the virus didn't activate until I tried to open another program. I'll bet he uploaded it directly onto my computer while I was in the bathroom."

"Why onto your computer?" Austin was unconvinced. "You said the virus could have been uploaded onto any terminal in the facility."

Dirk's eyes widened as understanding caused his already pasty skin to pale further. "My computer is the only one that could have allowed someone access to the blueprints for H5-40."

"Aren't backups of those plans stored on the network? Anyone can get to them."

"Yes, but they're encrypted and password protected. Only Al and I can open them."

"So you're saying that when you logged on today, you entered a password to read the files?"

"Yes. I was working on them not long before I left. I closed the blueprint but it was still readable because I hadn't logged off."

"And you left your computer unlocked?" Austin looked astonished Dirk had made such a careless mistake.

"Yes." Heat spread upward from the technician's collar. How could he have been so stupid?

"And you think Rylan came in here while you were in the bathroom, downloaded the blueprints and then uploaded the virus?"

"It's the only logical explanation."

Dirk and Austin held eye contact. Dirk contemplated the ramifications if this was what had truly happened. Someone was going to die, and he preferred it to be Rylan and not him. If they did not get those blueprints back immediately, their buyer would become hostile. Even if they managed to escape their client, if Rylan had found them out, then there would be a jail cell with their names on it.

"You know what this means, don't you?" Austin brought up the distasteful subject.

Dirk stared at him grimly. "Hunting time."

Unfortunately it was the only way.

~

Rylan listened to the conversation going on in Dirk's laboratory through the bug he had planted, which was feeding directly into his laptop. He was glad he was recording every word. At the same time he was afraid. He could not let them find the blueprints, especially if he wanted to stay alive.

"I had a little talk with our visitors." Albert popped his head into Rylan's office. "They have agreed to keep what they've seen to themselves."

Rylan removed the headphones that were plugged into his laptop. "Does Eric know?"

"Yes, he is allowing me to drive them home. It's the same kids H5-40 ran into the other day. I remembered when I showed you the pictures we retrieved from the hawk's memory, that you said you knew the girl. She is one of our guests."

Rylan sighed in exasperation. "I might have known she would disregard my warning."

"Your warning?" Albert was curious. "Who is she?"

"My niece. I became her guardian when my brother died three years ago."

Albert's brows rose in surprise. "I didn't know you lived with anyone."

"I don't." Rylan frowned with displeasure. "She's a delinquent. She comes and goes whenever she pleases and no matter what I try to do, she seems bent on throwing her life away."

Albert appeared even more surprised at this revelation. "She seems like such a nice girl."

"Looks can be deceiving. Take the boys, Al, and I'll deal with her."

Albert studied his colleague, compassion written across his features. From earlier conversations, Rylan knew he was a father, albeit his children were now fully grown. Rylan effected a dejected expression.

"We do all we can to raise them well, but sometimes they still choose a detrimental path no matter how hard we try."

"I think you're right." Rylan stood and gathered his keys and briefcase, knowing this was the perfect escape. "You go ahead and take the boys. I'll be along in a moment to fetch Laina."

"Alright." Albert nodded kindly and left the room.

Rylan hurriedly burned the recording from his computer onto another disc. He took out an envelope and dropped the three discs into it. He could not afford to be caught carrying these.

He sealed the envelope and went to the front desk. His hunch had been correct. The teenagers' backpacks had been searched and then dumped at reception ready to be collected when they left. Rylan smiled charmingly at the receptionist, trying to conjure up her name from his vague memory.

"Kate?"

The stylish woman smiled with pleasure. "Yes."

Rylan mentally sighed with relief. "Dr. Jefferson will be driving our guests home now. Would you mind if I take them their packs?"

"You mean the intruders?"

"Yes. As it turns out they're just a bunch of curious kids. Somehow I think this whole ordeal has cured them of nosiness." Rylan offered an amused smile that had the desired effect.

Having turned from her computer to give him her full attention, the receptionist appeared to be reluctant to end the interaction. "Typical kids I suppose."

"I'll get these to their rightful owners so that your office won't be cluttered."

"Thank you. Would you like some help?"

"Thank you for the offer but I should be okay." Rylan took three packs on one arm and two on the other. He stopped at his office long enough to slip the envelope into one pack and to collect his briefcase, laptop and keys. Then he set off to find the kids.

He stopped by Eric's office on the way to explain his plans. Always won over by Rylan's easygoing manner and friendly nature, Eric agreed to let him leave early to deal with his errant niece. There was not much any of them could do until the virus was eradicated from the system.

~

Rylan entered the room where the group of trespassers was being held. Albert was just removing the last set of handcuffs.

"I'm sorry about all of this," he apologized.

"Here are your packs boys." Rylan dropped them by the door.

"So it's true," Nick stated, "you are working on the H5-40 project."

"Now how would you know a thing like that?" Rylan asked with deceptive calm.

Nick remained silent. Laina guessed he was unwilling to implicate her should Rylan decide to threaten her again.

"What can I say boys? You're far smarter than most. Regular detectives, wouldn't you say Al?" Rylan grinned for effect.

Albert smiled in return. However, the boys were not buying the act.

"Definitely. Although I am sure they will keep our deal. They are all good lads." Albert smiled kindly.

"I'm sure they are. Now, Laina honey, you and I

have a long drive home and much to talk about." Rylan's expression was a mixture of affection and fatherly disapproval.

Laina saw right through it.

"You mean much to threaten her about," Logan replied, coldly eyeing him.

Rylan frowned in apparent confusion. "What are you talking about?"

"I'm talking about the way you choked and threatened her when she asked you about your involvement in the H5-40 project," Zach explained, his gaze just as hostile as Logan's.

"Threatened her?" Rylan stared at Laina, his expression wounded. "You've been making up lies again, haven't you?"

"Bruises don't lie, Mr. Jackson," Nick quietly asserted, gently taking Laina's wrist and holding it out for inspection.

Albert's gaze went from the nasty bruising on her arm to Rylan in disbelief. He seemed inclined to believe Rylan, although her wrist looked suspiciously like a large hand had grabbed it with tremendous force. Laina was frozen in place. She was beginning to feel numb from the inside out.

Rylan rubbed his face wearily and his next words were laced with resignation. "Here we go again. Every time it's the same. You get into trouble and suddenly I'm labeled the abusive uncle."

Doubt clouded Nick's face momentarily.

"Come on, Laina, let's go home." Rylan looked utterly defeated. "We'll talk about this in the car." He took steps toward her.

Wil moved sideways a couple of paces, positioning himself between them. Rylan stopped, looking slightly annoyed.

"I'm not going to hurt her." His tone was kind. "I don't know what lies she's told you, but there is no way I would hurt my own niece, or anyone else for that matter."

Wil would not budge. Logan and Zach stepped forward, one on either side of Wil. Nick put a protective hand on Laina's shoulder. Rylan stood a few inches taller than the boys and he met her gaze over their heads. Something flickered in his eyes that Laina did not like. Impatience, or was it fear?

"Look, I don't have time for all of this fuss. I don't want to have to pull rank but I will." Rylan's voice had grown stern.

"You're welcome to try. You're strong, there's no doubt about that." Logan measured Laina's uncle with a sliding glance. "But with four of us and one of you, I'm sure we could take you."

"Now boys, this is getting out of hand," Albert intervened, his eyes going from Laina's protective friends to his colleague. "Rylan is the girl's uncle and I can assure you he means no harm."

"You don't know him like we do," Zach answered the inventor before turning a hard stare upon Rylan.

"Look boys, we can do this the easy way or the hard way. Let me take Laina now or I'll call security."

Logan's cold gaze never wavered from Rylan Jackson's face. Laina wondered if he might be remembering a similar stand-off. She didn't know exactly what had transpired in his home, but she knew from the grapevine that he had often stood between his enraged father and his half beaten mother.

"Then you better call security, because we're not moving and you're not taking her."

Laina recalled the rough handling the guards had given the boys earlier. She also vividly remembered staring down those gun barrels. She wanted her friends to be able to leave peaceably, rather than have security go nuts again and possibly press charges.

She stepped from behind her loyal bodyguards. "I appreciate what you're trying to do guys, but it's best I go with my uncle."

"No Laina." Zach took her by the hand and held her back. "I'm not going to let him hurt you again."

"And I'm not going to let all of you get into deeper trouble because of me. I'm going." Laina tugged on her hand and Zach released her.

"Then we'll stop by your place as soon as we get back," Nick announced.

"Yeah, and if there's so much as a scratch on her we'll go see Sheriff Hackett," Logan threatened.

Rylan sighed. "Boys, you're totally misguided, but you're all more than welcome to stop by. I'll have the kettle boiling ready for a round of coffees." He beckoned to Laina. "Come on, honey."

"You can dispense with the pet names, Uncle Rylan," Laina informed him quietly. "You and I both know you wish I wasn't born." She walked straight past him and out into the corridor, totally unimpressed by his act. She was willing to forgive and even to love him, but no longer would she play along with his lies.

"We'll stop by your house as soon as we get home, Laina," Zach called after her.

"I'd appreciate that." She passed a grateful glance before Rylan closed the door behind them.

~

The scientist's car followed them for the first five miles until Rylan got a flat tire. The other car pulled abreast of him as he got out to survey the damage. Laina stuck her head out her window and glanced toward the rear right wheel.

"Punctured!" Rylan muttered angrily. "Austin Keffler!" He hurriedly set about changing the flat.

"You need a hand?" Albert called across the front passenger seat through the open window, past where Nick was sitting.

"No, I should be alright. This will only take a couple of minutes. You go ahead." Rylan waved him on.

"Are you sure?"

"Positive. We'll be fine."

"Okay then."

Albert put the car in gear and continued down the track. The boys in the backseat turned to stare anxiously out the rear window.

Laina watched as they disappeared from sight. She absently wondered what would become of their bikes, which were still parked in the woods. It was an odd thing to worry about considering her circumstance. Yet strangely enough God's peace hedged her in like a wall of protection. Her fear of Rylan, and of any man for that matter, was gone. No matter what happened today, no one would be able to steal her faith or her relationship with Jesus Christ. She was eternally secure.

Rylan finished with the tire and climbed back in. He looked anxiously behind them and it was then it occurred to Laina he was expecting to be followed.

It dawned on her that he had used her as a means of escape. Had he caused the computer crash? She mentally shook herself. It was better not to think about it.

Rylan put the car in gear and planted his foot on the accelerator. The wheels kicked up stones and dust. They drove for another thirty minutes before the faint sound of rotor blades slicing through dry summer air disturbed the otherwise quiet afternoon. The sound grew increasingly louder, finally drowning out the car engine as it roared along the dirt track.

About eighty yards ahead a shiny blue helicopter with the Astro Enterprises logo on the side suddenly descended from the sky, landing directly in the center of the road.

Rylan muttered under his breath and jammed on the brakes. Memories of another collision long ago flashed through Laina's mind and she drew a deep breath and braced herself for what she knew was coming.

The brakes locked and the back of the vehicle fish-tailed. The car skidded for another sixty yards before the back left panel slammed heavily into a tree, abruptly ending the out of control ride. The impact jarred them both and the air bags activated.

Laina gasped, winded and in shock. She unbuckled her seatbelt and wrenched open her door. She stumbled onto the road in a daze, glancing back at the vehicle that was semi-wrapped around a tree trunk. Her gaze then swung to the helicopter that was perched like a large bird of prey only twenty yards away. From its backseat a figure emerged. His black curly hair danced wildly in the wind whipped up by the propellers, and in his hand he clutched a pistol aimed directly at them.

14

Rylan stumbled out of the car and glared angrily at Austin Keffler. "Have you lost your mind? You nearly got us killed! Now look at my car!"

"I should think your car is the least of your problems right now," Austin yelled over the deafening whine of the engine and rotor blades. His pistol was aimed at Rylan's chest.

"What are you talking about? And why are you pointing a gun at me?"

Laina watched the standoff in a state of shock. She was almost glad for her uncle's amazing acting abilities. He was playing the part of confused, maltreated colleague quite well. He deserved an Oscar award.

"We both know why I'm here, Jackson. Get in." Austin indicated the helicopter with a nod of his head and then waved his pistol at Laina. "You too."

Laina looked to her uncle for direction. Should she comply? Rylan nodded for her to obey and he started toward Keffler. Laina followed him.

The gunman stepped aside and allowed his two

captives to precede him into the back of the helicopter. When they were seated, Austin climbed aboard
and took the opposite seat, his back to the pilot. He
slid the door closed and buckled his lap belt. The
pilot glanced at his passengers, his expression unreadable, and then turned his attention to the instru-
mentation in front of him. How had Austin procured
his cooperation, and the helicopter from Eric for that
matter?

"Take off!" Austin tossed over his shoulder. "You
know where to go."

The metal bird lifted off the ground in a swirl of
dust. Laina stared out the glass window in the door
to her left. They were not headed toward any major
towns. In fact, they were flying further into the hostile, uninhabited mountains that stretched for hundreds of miles in each direction.

Rylan studied the CIA agent carefully and must
have seen there was no use pretending. "Where are
we going?"

Austin was dispassionate. "To a place where no
one will find your dead body."

"You can't kill me." Rylan affected a smug smile.
"Or you'll never find the blueprints."

Austin's stare was hard and cold. "Then I suggest
you tell me where they are."

"Do you think I'm stupid? The second you get what

you want I'm a dead man. There's no way I'm telling you where I've hidden them until you set this thing down."

"Well then, let's play a little guessing game." Austin's calm spoke volumes. The traitorous CIA agent was getting a great amount of sadistic pleasure from having the upper hand.

Laina glanced at the trees whisking by as the helicopter hugged the contours of the land. Why were they flying so low? Was it to make their escape less visible? Should she put her belt on too? She returned her wide-eyed stare to the reprehensible character still holding his gun on them.

God help us, please?

Be anxious for nothing. I am your light and your salvation. Who should you be afraid of? The comforting words dropped into her thoughts from an outside source.

Okay God, I choose to trust You. Whether I live or die, I pray You'll glorify Your name. Laina silently surrendered her life.

"The blueprints won't be in your car because you're not that stupid. You wouldn't have left them at work. So that leaves only one more option. They must be on you."

Rylan's composure was excellent. "Nice try, but no."

Austin's eyes narrowed dangerously. "You wouldn't dare e-mail them. Our server keeps a record of all staff e-mails."

"You mean the record my virus just destroyed?"

"Who did you send the blueprints to?"

Rylan remained silent.

"I *will* find out. Dirk is able to work magic with those computers."

"You're assuming Dirk is smarter than I am."

Austin shrugged. "It's of no consequence either way. I'll just kill her instead." He aimed his pistol across the small space at Laina's head. With his free hand he slid the door open again.

"Why are you doing that?" Laina nervously gripped the seat beneath her with both hands. She did not like how close she was to the edge... and those trees.

"The door is open so I can dispose of your body," Austin explained callously.

Laina's horrified gaze snapped to her uncle to see what he would do. He had declared his contempt for her on so many occasions that she had lost count. But in that moment as Austin's weapon was trained upon her, panic entered Rylan's eyes. Laina was stunned to realize that beneath his resentment, he actually cared.

Rylan lunged and made a grab for the gun. Laina ducked at the same time, burying her head in her lap.

The pistol discharged into the wall above her. The pilot exclaimed in fright and the helicopter slowed and tilted up and then left with a surprised jerk of his hands upon the stick.

Laina grasped for something to stop her from toppling out. She tumbled through the doorway and her fingers latched onto the metal strip the door slid along. She glanced down as her legs dangled midair. Another shot rang out above the sound of the helicopter blades.

The pilot slowed the helicopter to a hover, continuously glancing over his shoulder in alarm to see what was happening in the rear seats. It was obvious he wanted to land and get away from the madness, only the terrain below them was dense with forest. The trees were so tightly packed together, it was doubtful even light could slip between them.

The two men in the back continued to grapple for the gun, discharging a third bullet. The panicked pilot ducked and then the bird tilted again. Laina was suspended for several more seconds before her fingers lost their precarious grip. Her heart leapt into her throat with the terrifying sensation of free falling. She plummeted down, down, screaming.

"Laina, no!" She heard Rylan's voice fade into the blue expanse as she dropped away from the open doorway.

A large spruce broke her fall, branches bending and buckling, snapping and scraping. Unfortunately more things snapped than branches. Pain shot through Laina's right leg moments before her head collided with a solid lower branch. She landed like a rag doll upon the forest floor, knocked mercifully unconscious.

~

"But Sheriff, it's four thirty and they're still not home!" Zach pointed out. "We all left the lab just after one thirty. It only took us an hour to drive back."

"Yeah," Nick agreed, "they're three hours late. Doesn't that seem suspicious to you?"

The four boys had gone straight to Sheriff Hawkins when it became apparent Rylan was not going to show up. The sheriff had urged them to stay put and had driven over to Rylan's house. He waited half an hour before coming back. Now they were in the sheriff's office debating what to do next.

"Why don't we take a drive out there?" Dan Fisher suggested, for once taking the boys' side.

Zach watched him study Wil's mounting distress and noted a disturbed crease knit his brows. It could not be denied that something had gone terribly wrong today, even if the two lawmen refused to believe the teenagers' outrageous story about a secret lab in the middle of the national park. Zach supposed that Wil's cooperation with Logan and Nick in one of their schemes, spoke volumes.

Sheriff Hawkins' lips thinned as his gaze narrowed in thought. Zach guessed his displeased mood had something to do with the uneasy feeling that trouble was afoot on his turf.

"Alright, but you boys had better not be pulling my chain!" He pointed a warning finger at the teenagers, his stern gaze clearly communicating that he would not be trifled with.

Nick and Wil shook their heads, assuring him that they were telling the truth.

"Then let's go. Dan, will you stick around until I get back? Radio me if there's a problem. If anything happens locally and you need backup then call the office in Walkerville." The sheriff grabbed his hat and keys off his desk and headed for the front entrance.

"Will do."

~

Sheriff Hawkins cast a stern glance at the boys sitting in his car champing at the bit to get out. They reluctantly stayed put.

He circled the expensive red sports car on foot. The back panel had well and truly wrapped itself around a tree. The engine had been switched off, although the keys were still dangling from the ignition. The air bags had deflated and now hung limply inside the vehicle. Tucked behind the back seat was a laptop in its padded bag, as well as a briefcase. The right passenger door had been left open and lying on the floor was a wallet. Sheriff Hawkins guessed that it had been flung across the car upon impact. The driver side door was also hanging open.

He was puzzled. There was no doubt that this was Rylan Jackson's car. It appeared that he had braked hard, as indicated by the snaking trail left in the dirt. He had obviously lost control and then crashed. Why had he left his wallet, briefcase and laptop?

He and his passenger had gotten out immediately after impact and then abandoned the scene. Where could they have gone? Had someone picked them up on their way past? Had they walked into the forest? There was no blood on the interior of the car, which afforded the sheriff a measure of relief. However, that did not mean that no one had been hurt.

He decided to radio Dan for reinforcements. They had an accident scene, and if Rylan and Laina had not already shown up in Icy Creek or Walkerville, then it was also possible that they had missing persons.

~

A dull throbbing sensation nudged Laina's awareness until she awoke. She opened heavy eyelids and blinked slowly. Her face was pressed into a bed of pine needles and the landscape around her was growing dark.

Final rays of warm sunlight tried valiantly to pierce the thick stand of pines, which were nestled closely together as though afraid of the darkness creeping in. Yet the light failed to touch the forest floor. A cool draft snaked through the undergrowth and brought goose bumps to Laina's flesh. Where was she?

She shifted slightly, intending to slowly sit up. Tendrils of agony shot up her right leg and her left ankle protested sharply. She gasped and lay still on her side. She felt bruised all over and her head was pounding. She had to get help, or at the very least assess the damage.

Keeping her legs still, she rose on one elbow. Her head swam and she felt like she was going to be sick. However, she forced herself to look. Her left ankle was blue and swollen, and her right shin had an unnatural indentation two inches long. It had been broken in two places and knocked slightly inward. Her arms and legs were covered in dried blood from gashes and grazes, and her t-shirt had torn. Blood had seeped through onto her clothing from scratches

169

to her torso.

How long had she been lying here? Long enough for blood to dry, she supposed. She told herself she needed to do something about her leg. Yet her thoughts were hazy and all she wanted to do was pass out or be sick. She gave in to dizziness and sank back onto the ground into unconsciousness.

15

It was close to midnight as Zach dropped onto the couch at home and rubbed tired, scratchy eyes. He could not sleep. Not when Laina was out there somewhere.

There was still no sign of Rylan or his niece. Sheriff Hawkins had called in search crews from far and wide. Yet after hours of hunting they had come up empty. There were no tracks, no scent to follow; absolutely nothing had been left behind. It was almost as if they had disappeared off the face of the planet.

A sudden barrage of traffic coming from the direction the four teenagers had claimed was a secret laboratory, had clearly caught the sheriff's interest. He questioned passers-by who said yes, they knew Rylan, but no, they did not know what had become of him that afternoon.

That was when something very strange happened. A black helicopter had set down in the middle of the road and men in dark suits climbed out. The boys had exchanged glances and Sheriff Hawkins narrowed his gaze suspiciously. FBI? CIA? The simple crash took on a whole new dimension.

Dan, who had come on the scene not long after Sheriff Hawkins, had driven the boys back to town. There they took up residence in the sheriff's office, waiting for any kind of news.

It was around ten that night when Zach phoned his mom and a very worried Caroline Delaney had come to fetch him. She'd kindly dropped Logan, Nick and Wil off to their anxious families before taking her son home for a good chewing out. Now she was in bed asleep and Zach was suffering insomnia.

He stared into the dark living room and mentally berated himself. When he was done berating himself, he had a go at God.

A board in the hallway creaked and then the kitchen light flicked on.

"Zach?"

"In here, Mom." Zach's voice was subdued.

Caroline padded into the living room in bare feet wearing her crazy pink pajamas with little frowning cartoon cows on them. Written sporadically between the bovines were the words 'grumpy cow'. Zach remembered the day she had brought them home, proudly putting on a fashion parade for him. He had thought that her disgustingly cheerful personality was entirely the opposite of those grumpy little cows, but the zany pajamas somehow suited her.

She spotted him on the couch and her compassionate eyes looked directly into his soul. "Can't sleep?"

"I feel sick to my stomach," he admitted, aware she could already see that. "I should have trusted my instincts. I never should have let her leave with him."

Caroline sat on the couch with her son, slouching down beside him and stretching her legs out in front of her as he was doing. "You can't blame yourself. She chose to go."

"Because she was protecting us. If Rylan hadn't threatened to call security she would have stayed, I know it."

"Then blame Rylan, but don't blame yourself."

Zach turned his head on the couch cushion to look thoughtfully at his mother. "The one I really blame is God."

Caroline surprised him. "I know you do. You've been doing that for a very long time. It's not God's fault your father got cancer, Zach. God didn't create disease."

"Laina said roughly the same thing," Zach mused and stared blankly across the room again.

"You know, I look at your father's death as a miraculous healing," Caroline shared for the first time. "He stepped from his mortal body, which had wrapped him in pain for so long, into eternity where there is no more suffering or tears or agony. God healed him. He gave him a new body and freed him from cancer." Caroline's voice grew unsteady with emotion, yet Zach could also hear hope and joy in it as well.

He glanced at her again. "I never thought of it that way."

"Me either. Not until God took me to Revelation chapter twenty-one."

Zach was curious. "When was that?"

"Just before we moved here."

Zach looked away. It was a nice thought, God healing his father in that way. But it did not make Zach any less angry with his Maker. He did not like God's solution one bit. He wanted his father back and that was the bottom line.

"So," Caroline went back to Zach's admission, "you're blaming God for what's happened to Laina."

"She's a Christian, Mom, just like you. She trusts God to look after her and all He's ever done is take away the people she loves."

"What does she have to say about it?"

"She says God lets people make the choices they want to, even decisions that affect others negatively. She says the bad stuff that's happened to her has been people's fault, not God's."

"She's right. I'll bet she also said at some point that God has a way of bringing good out of bad." Caroline

174

gently nudged Zach with an elbow, her coaxing smile once again contradicting her grumpy cow pajamas.

Zach reluctantly smiled, but only to make his mother feel better. He still felt awful. Especially with such an unpredictable God in control, and worse yet, men like Rylan Jackson roaming scot-free.

~

Laina was too out of it to be afraid of the night noises around her; the rustling, the dense blackness where even the moon was unable to penetrate, the distant howl of a wolf and other nocturnal animals roaming about. She was oblivious. However, with the dawn of a new day came concerns of an entirely different nature.

Laina awoke as the sun was steadily climbing in the brilliant summer sky. Every part of her was sore, yet thankfully her head seemed to have cleared. She managed to pull herself into an upright position, although it left her gasping for breath from the pain.

Splinting her right leg was not an option. Although there were sticks nearby, she had nothing with which to bind them to her leg. She reassessed her left ankle and decided it had to be sprained, at the very least.

She considered bottom shuffling to get help, then thought of how dangerous that could be. She would only get herself even more lost. Then there was the issue of food. She had not eaten since breakfast the day before, and with this heat she was becoming increasingly thirsty.

She leaned against a solid tree trunk and decided to wait it out. What if Rylan was able to get help? He might know her rough location. But then if he knew where she was, then so did Austin. That chilling thought sent a shudder down her spine. What if one of those gunshots had killed her uncle? Pain constricted her chest.

Laina began to pray, and as she did, a heavenly calm descended over her. She felt God very close, closer than she had ever felt Him before. She sensed his guardian angels around her, as real as the trees towering above her. So she rested her head against the trunk and settled in to wait.

~

"Any news?" Logan asked Dan Fisher the next day, waiting eagerly on the other side of the counter.

"Sorry son." Dan's expression was filled with regret. "Search and Rescue have been combing the forest all night. So far they haven't found a thing."

"But there's still hope, right?" Logan's eyes pleaded desperately for assurance.

Dan forced a smile. "Of course. They didn't have a full day to search yesterday, but today they do. It'll be a lot easier in daylight."

Logan sighed with relief. "Okay. Will you call me when you hear something?"

This time Dan's smile was genuine. "I'll do that. Half the town has been ringing wanting to know about Laina. Rest assured that you're at the top of my list, right along with Gracie, Zach, Nick and Wil."

"Thanks Dan." Logan offered a partial smile that did not quite reach his eyes, and trudged dejectedly from the office. He felt powerless just waiting.

Sheriff Hawkins and then those men in dark suits had reiterated over and over again that there was nothing he could do. He would only be in the way. That made Logan furious. He may not be an adult yet, but that did not mean he couldn't be of use. He knew those woods like the back of his hand and so did Nick and Wil. Logan decided to drop in on Wil. He much preferred to wait for news with a friend than all alone.

~

By the end of day two, the news of Rylan and Laina's disappearance had spread throughout the entire town. Search teams continued an around the clock hunt for the missing pair, becoming increasingly disappointed and frustrated with their fruitless efforts. Meanwhile townspeople talked and worried and waited anxiously for any kind of report. None came. Day three arrived and with it sprang new hope. Surely today was the day?

Sheriff Hawkins walked miserably into his office that evening and slumped in his chair. Self-recrimination was written all over him.

The four boys who had been sitting in the waiting area all afternoon had stood upon his entrance. They noticed his disheartened demeanor and had their answer. She was still missing.

They had overheard people talking. Three days in the wilderness with this heat, without food or water, did not afford good odds.

They wordlessly left and wandered down the street, hands stuffed in pockets and eyes downcast. With unspoken accord they walked toward Rylan's house.

Zach supposed it was some irrepressible surge of hope that just maybe she might be there. They had already checked her tree house twice that day only to be repeatedly disappointed.

Dusk was coming on and with it a gentle breeze blew in, gradually dropping the temperature. Daylight faded away.

"Hey, look at that!" Nick suddenly broke the silence and pointed down the street.

They were only a couple of houses away from Rylan's stone mansion. Even from that distance, Zach could see light emanating from the front yard. People were milling about on the footpath, all of them quiet and subdued. Some were coming, some were going and some were just standing. The boys approached and nudged through the crowd to gain a curious glimpse of the house.

Zach drew in a sharp breath as he beheld hundreds of candles lining the footpath to the veranda. Bundles of flowers and cards were strewn across the manicured lawn.

Logan silently fumed. Zach understood his anger toward the people who would go to such kind extremes for the monster who had deceived them all. Yet when he began reading the cards and notes attached to the bunches of flowers, he saw they were for Laina.

"Look at how many lives she's touched," Nick commented softly as he took in the amazing show of love and support from the people of Icy Creek.

Wil's eyes filled with tears that spilled onto his cheeks. That he liked Laina and considered her a good friend was evident. He said nothing, and yet as always, his open expression said it all.

Zach felt deep loss well up within him. Their last conversation sprang to mind unbidden.

"You're angry at God for what He allowed when you let Him take charge of your life. As a result you've pushed Him away and now you're trying to control it yourself, only it's not working. You're angry, scared, empty and restless."

"Just shut up Laina! What do you know about me?"

"I used to be where you are." Laina's eyes softened with compassion.

"But now you've got it all figured out, haven't you?"

"I don't think I'm better than you, if that's what you're getting at. I only brought it up because I can see you're so unhappy and I know if you'll go to Jesus He'll give you peace. Then you won't have to carry the burden that comes with running your own life."

"My life is just fine the way it is."

"Then sit down and relax. Prove to me that your way works better than mine. Show me that trusting yourself gives you peace and maybe I'll be convinced."

Tears blurred Zach's vision and he felt a powerful presence tugging at his heart. "She was right."

"Right about what?" Logan walked across the lawn to Zach's side.

"She said I'd pushed God away because I didn't like

what had happened when He was in control of my life." Zach was honest. His gaze drifted over the candles and flowers.

"She actually said that to you?" Nick half smiled. Zach nodded.

"What happened when God was in control of your life?" Wil asked curiously.

"My dad died." Zach briefly met his friend's sad gaze.

"I'm sorry, Zach."

"What was it that made her so different?" Logan wondered aloud. "I mean, I wasn't always nice to her, but she seemed to see straight through me. I've always wondered why she never gave up being kind."

"It was her relationship with God," Wil answered.

His friends looked at him enquiringly. People continued to mill around them but they no longer noticed. The certainty in Wil's tone had caught their attention.

"What makes you say that?" Nick was the one to ask the question in each pair of eyes.

"She told me about Jesus once in Math class. She said He was her best friend and she couldn't imagine life without Him. She said that when Jesus gave His life, it was like a gift I could accept and unwrap."

"You know," Nick remarked thoughtfully, "I always wondered what those Christians were on about when they talked about salvation and all that. But whatever Laina's got is real."

"I don't know about you guys," Zach broke into the discussion, feeling a growing sense of urgency, "but I know I can't do this anymore."

"Do what?" Logan puzzled.

"Life. I can't control what happens anymore than you can. I've hit rock bottom and I'm desperate. I can't see any other way out. I need God and I'm so tired of fighting Him."

Nick's brows rose in surprise at such an open and honest admission.

"Me too. What do I have to do?" Logan asked softly.

"Well that's just it," Wil added thoughtfully, "from what Laina shared, you don't have to do anything. She said that no one can be good enough for God on their own. She said we're always falling short of His standards. That's why He sent His Son Jesus to pay the cost of our wrongdoing. I think she said the cost was death, or something like that."

"She did. She was quoting the Bible. It says that people who have sinned must die and be separated from God forever in hell to pay for those sins. It also says that those who believe Jesus took their punishment, can be friends with Him forever and go to heaven when they die," Zach explained, feeling bad for having had this knowledge and rejected it.

"So I just believe and that's it?" Logan clarified.

"Sort of. You also have to tell God you're sorry for the bad stuff you've said and done. Then ask to be His friend."

A combination of desperation, the pain of his past and the shame of the sin he carried inside of him, showed in Logan's expression as he let down his guard completely for the first time in his teenage life. "Let's do it."

"It worked for Laina," Wil reasoned. "She was the most joyful person I've ever met. If Jesus can do that in her after all she'd been through, then I want Him in my life too."

"And what about you Nick?" Zach looked questioningly at his friend.

A resolute gleam entered Nick's eyes and his hands suddenly began to tremble nervously. "I'm in."

Surrounded by prayerful townsfolk, the four boys stood in a huddle outside Rylan Jackson's home and raised a prayer of their own. It was not eloquent, but it was heartfelt and life changing. As four more souls surrendered their lives to God, heaven rejoiced.

16

The darkness closed in on all sides like a suffocating blanket. Night sounds drifted in and out of Laina's foggy awareness. Fear of what might be lurking in the dense forest around her was overridden by the hunger gnawing at her stomach. Her mouth was parched, and the pain in her leg a constant throbbing sensation.

She had waited patiently the first day to be rescued. No one had come. Unquenchable thirst drove her to seek water the next day. She had quickly discovered that her sprained ankle would not support her weight. She had attempted crawling and found that it severely aggravated her broken leg. As a result, she had resorted to shuffling backward on her bottom, using her hands and arms to pull her along. It was a torturous and tedious method. All the same, it was the best she could do.

By the end of day two she was exhausted and suffering dehydration. During the night when the cold had descended through the trees, coating the ground with damp droplets, Laina had felt inexplicably hot. The cold had seeped into her bones. Still she sweated. She then went from sweating to shivering, continuously alternating between the two extremes.

It was in the light of day three that she understood why. Her right leg was swollen and the gashes on that leg in particular had started to weep. Her leg was infected.

Yet she shuffled on, continuing her dogged pursuit of water. What little daylight that had found its way to the forest floor was now fading quickly. Day three was coming to a close and still there was no sign of help.

Laina stopped just below a rise and panted from exertion. The world around her seemed to swim and her thoughts were an incoherent muddle. She felt so weak. All she knew was that if she didn't drink soon, she would die.

Please God, I need water. It was when she stopped praying that a faint trickling sound penetrated the haze surrounding her brain. In excited desperation she bottom shuffled to the top of the rise.

Glancing over her shoulder she saw the source of the sound. There below the rise in a shallow gully, flanked on either side by youthful native trees, ran a small creek. Laina half shuffled and half slid down the embankment, not caring that the skin on her palms was blistered and bleeding or that her leg and ankle were sending out agonized protests.

The instant she reached the water she immersed her mouth and drank deeply. After her initial thirst abated she sank onto the ground and lay there exhausted.

"Thank you Lord Jesus," she breathed and stared blankly up into the canopy above her, slowly blinking heavy eyelids.

Daylight gradually vanished and a chill wind swept through the trees, its icy breath bringing goose bumps to her flesh and starting her shivering all over again.

She dragged herself a little higher up the small gully and covered herself with dry leaves for warmth. In the distance a mountain lion gave a terrifying growl. Laina huddled into the slope and her bed of leaves as fear crept in on stealthy paws.

I will lift up my eyes to the hills, familiar words drifted through her tortured thoughts, soothing and calming her soul. She recognized them from Psalm one-hundred and twenty-one. *From whence comes my help? My help comes from the Lord, who made heaven and earth. He will not allow your foot to be moved; He who keeps you will not slumber. Behold, He who keeps Israel shall neither slumber nor sleep. The Lord is your keeper; the Lord is your shade at your right hand. The sun shall not strike you by day, nor the moon by night. The Lord shall preserve you from all evil; He shall preserve your soul. The Lord shall preserve your going out and your coming in from this time forth, and even forevermore.*

Accompanying the psalm was a presence, powerful, comforting and almost tangible. Laina felt that if she reached out she would be able to feel the texture of His cloak that now sheltered her. Although she knew in reality that it was a spiritual covering. He was a secure shield against night predators and Laina was able to give in to the weariness overpowering her body, knowing that the God who did not sleep would watch over her.

~

"Mom, what's all this stuff doing on my bed?" Zach called across the hallway.

His mother was propped against a stack of pillows reading in her room. It had to be around midnight, and just like Zach, she could not sleep. News of his and his friends' decision to follow Jesus that very evening had been so exciting. Yet clearly nagging at the back of her mind was Laina's disappearance. It was the same for Zach.

"Your backpack was dirty so I tossed it in the wash

with the towels." Caroline's eyes never left the pages before her.

"Oh." Zach stared at the pile of miscellaneous junk on his bed. "Thanks." He did not feel thankful, but for once he heeded Laina's admonition to show respect and appreciation to his mother.

He finally saw in her what Laina had seen. Caroline was not selfishly trying to please herself or to ruin his life. She was just trying to do what she thought was best. He was now willing to admit that the move from New York had been a good choice.

As Zach sifted through the bits and pieces, he pondered the way God had used the people in this little town to bring him to life and back into His family. At the top of this list of people was Laina Jackson.

Zach threw a four day old sandwich in the bin and tossed an empty drink bottle in the kitchen sink. He returned to his room to sort through the last of the items. He got to the bottom of the pile and frowned. What was an unmarked envelope doing in his bag? Where had it come from? Or better yet, what was in it?

Zach curiously peeled the sealed flap and dumped the contents on his bed. His puzzled frown deepened. Three discs, all of them miniature. One was clearly labeled 'virus'. The other two were unmarked.

Zach booted up his computer, impatiently waiting

for the desktop image to appear. He sat at his desk and stared at the discs curiously while he waited, turning them over in his fingers.

Virus... No way! His sleepy mind kicked into gear. *Surely this isn't the virus that wiped the laboratory computers?*

The desktop image with all of his program icons finally appeared on the screen. Zach inserted one of the unlabeled discs into the disc drive. The computer recognized an audio file and automatically opened a program to play it. He listened at first with confusion and then realization hit him full force. There were two voices, one of whom was Austin Keffler. The other was unfamiliar.

"How do you think the virus got into the system?" Austin asked.

"I can't be sure. It could have been uploaded onto the network from any computer in the facility."

"And you don't think it got into the system when someone accessed the internet?"

"No. Our firewall is too strong. We've got more protection than most government agencies do. Whoever did this was from the inside."

"Sabotage? Who would want to do that?"

Zach heard the tapping of computer keys in the background.

"My guess is that someone is onto us and wanted

to prevent the software from being stolen."

"Albert Jefferson?" Austin speculated.

"Al? Not a chance. He's too trusting to ever think someone from here would steal his designs."

"If not Albert then who?" Austin sounded puzzled.

The keyboard suddenly went quiet.

"Rylan Jackson. He's the only other person here with the ability to create a virus that could circumnavigate our antivirus protection. I forgot he used to design antivirus software at his previous company. He once told me he used to invent viruses to test the programs he put together, and I saw him walking past the lab on my way to the bathroom. He was the only person around at the time."

Zach's mind reeled as he listened to the rest of the discussion. The final words spoken haunted him.

Hunting time.

Had Rylan Jackson stolen the designs to protect them from being illegally sold by two traitors? Perhaps he wasn't the bad guy after all. Then that left Austin Keffler and the other man on this recording whom he had called Dirk.

Did Dr. Jefferson and the people at the lab know they had a thief in their midst, or was Rylan being blamed? Worse yet, if the two bad guys were aware that Rylan knew what they were up to, and apparently they did, then his disappearance was possibly foul play. And embroiled in the middle of this mess was Laina, an innocent bystander. Zach had to tell the boys. No, he had to tell Sheriff Hawkins. Wait! He had to tell Dr. Jefferson!

Zach leapt to his feet and was about to dash for the phone when he remembered the other disc in his possession. He sat back down and ejected the previous one from his computer. He then inserted the disc in his hand.

A new program automatically installed itself and then images flooded the screen before his eyes, flooring him speechless. It was the hawk. Every tiny detail. Each code and sequence, all of the testing data, the composition for the making of the outer casing. The whole shebang.

Zach's curiosity begged for him to fully explore this work of genius. On the other hand, his rational mind demanded he get this back to its owner. It would only bring his family and friends trouble, just as it had for Rylan. If the evil powers at work in this situation were aware that he possessed the plans for H5-40, they would no doubt kill him. What was one teenager in exchange for having a machine that could track an enemy with precision, stealth and speed, and then neutralize them?

Track with precision, stealth and speed... precision and speed... Zach's mind ground to a sudden halt. *Laina!*

What if Dr. Jefferson could use the plans to finish fixing H5-40 and then have it find Laina? After three days, numerous search and rescue teams, including trained air scenting dogs, were no closer to finding her than when they began. The area they needed to cover was simply too big. Many places were so inhospitable and inaccessible that without H5-40 they could never be reached. And if Austin Keffler truly was involved, then they needed to consider the possibility that Rylan and Laina may not even be in the wilderness.

"Mom, come look at this!"

Zach went to fetch the cordless phone.

~

"Oh come on!" Logan exclaimed in frustration early the next morning. "You've got to let us in!"

"I don't have to let anyone in, sonny," the security guard in the booth outside the laboratory replied through a small hole in the bulletproof glass.

His eyes were stern and his lips were set in a grim line. In his arms was a rather large and intimidating automatic weapon.

The boys knew that the other guards would not be far away. Their car was probably being watched even now. It would only take one word from this man in the booth and security would rain down on them in a torrential downpour.

Sheriff Hawkins was in the driver's seat, looking more than a little frustrated. "I have jurisdiction over this entire district!"

"Not over this facility you don't." The guard was adamant.

"Then I'll get a warrant."

"Good luck with that." The guard smiled smugly.

Zach leaned out the passenger window. "Tell Dr. Jefferson that Zach, Logan, Wil and Nick are here and that we know where the designs for H5-40 are. Tell him we know who took them and we have proof."

As he'd hoped, this gained the guard's undivided attention. At first the man frowned and then he narrowed his gaze suspiciously.

"Wait there a moment." He picked up a phone in the booth and talked for several minutes. The conversation was too soft for the visitors to hear. Finally he returned to the window.

"Drive through. Park your car out the front and walk through the entrance."

Sheriff Hawkins raised intrigued brows and muttered under his breath, "So H5-40 is the magic password."

17

They were ushered into a private, very modern office. A well dressed, rotund man sat behind a large black desk in a comfortable leather chair, a flat screen computer the focus of his attention. The interior of the room was a soft gray, with matching carpet. Flanking the wall behind the businessman was a tall black bookshelf laden with fat volumes.

The gentleman glanced up when the group of five entered his office. He leaned back in his chair, shrewd eyes measuring them over a hawkish nose.

There was another leather chair opposite the man behind the desk, which Sheriff Hawkins took. The boys were left to stand before this intimidating fellow, their curious eyes wandering the room and then resting upon his formidable face.

"What's this I hear about you knowing the whereabouts of the blueprints to H5-40?"

"I think Rylan Jackson stashed these discs in Zach's bag before he left this place. From the conversation he recorded on one of them, it's obvious he discovered that at least two of your employees are selling you out," Sheriff Hawkins briefly explained and held up the discs in an unmarked envelope.

"I've been led to believe he is the sell-out," the boss of Astro Enterprises replied.

"Here." Zach took the discs from the sheriff and handed over the one containing the recorded conversation. "Listen to this."

Eric complied, sliding the disc into his computer. His cagey expression soon transformed to one of boiling rage as he listened to two of his workers discussing their treacherous dealings.

"I should have known Keffler was up to no good when he convinced me to let him go after Jackson in my helicopter. He said he'd discovered evidence that Jackson was planning on selling the blueprints to a foreigner. When Keffler didn't return, I simply guessed that Jackson had taken him out." He indicated the miniature discs in Zach's hand. "And what of those other two?"

"The plans for H5-40 and the virus Rylan used to wipe the system to keep Austin and Dirk from stealing them. I think he stowed them in my pack because he realized Keffler knew that he was onto them, and Rylan didn't want Austin getting his hands on the hawk."

The entrepreneur held out a demanding hand, expecting Zach to pass them over.

Zach smiled. "I don't think so."

Eric's eyes narrowed dangerously. "Don't play games with me, boy."

"I'm not playing games. Thanks to the men that work for you, my best friend is missing, likely somewhere out there in that wilderness. We want her back."

Logan, Wil and Nick exchanged scheming smiles. Sheriff Hawkins was aware of their plan, and although he looked a little uncomfortable, he was desperate and would do whatever it took to find Laina.

"And what do you expect me to do?" Eric studied them with a displeased frown.

"Let us talk to Dr. Jefferson. If he can get the hawk working again using these blueprints, then we want him to use it to find Laina," Zach expounded.

"Absolutely out of the question!" The businessman shook his head vigorously.

The boys looked at each other anxiously. Zach refused to give in.

"Just think of the amazing opportunity it would be to fully test it."

"And have the world discover what we've created?"

"You have my word that your involvement in the search would remain strictly confidential," Sheriff

Jay .H. Dee

Hawkins entered the bargaining process.

"No, absolutely not!" Eric was unmovable.

Logan nodded to Sheriff Hawkins, encouraging him to enact plan B, which they had discussed in the car on their way. The sheriff rubbed his face with a weary hand, clearly reluctant to resort to dirty tactics. He swallowed his pride and ignored his conscience.

"Then you leave us with no other choice but to go public with this whole sordid thing."

"Yeah," Logan chipped in, "we'll tell them everything."

"Our run-ins with H5-40, the laboratory here, the way your security went nuts and nearly shot us when we were on public property," Zach continued.

"Not to mention Austin Keffler's involvement in the disappearance of Rylan and Laina Jackson," Nick interjected.

"And the biggest problem of all," Sheriff Hawkins added the clincher, "the way you've kept quiet through this whole investigation, when all along you've been fed information by the CIA."

Eric's face turned a mottled red, a testament to the volcano inside ready to explode. "What do you know of the CIA's involvement?"

Sheriff Hawkins slanted the entrepreneur a dry look. "I knew the CIA were involved when men in suits driving government cars showed up at a common car accident scene and practically took over. And besides, Keffler is CIA. I checked. "

"Yeah, get real," Zach added his piece. "When they started poking around it was obvious this is about something of national importance."

Eric sighed. He was beaten and he knew it. Zach understood his dilemma and watched him silently struggle. Jeopardize his secret work at Astro Enterprises with media attention, or covertly find a lost girl?

"Okay," he finally agreed. "But you must give me your word that you will keep silent about H5-40 and let the CIA deal with Keffler. At the moment they can't find him, but believe me when I tell you that they will."

Sheriff Hawkins nodded slowly. "All we want is the girl."

Eric stood and walked around his desk toward the door. "Then let's pay Dr. Jefferson a visit."

~

"How much longer, doc?" Zach asked impatiently.

Wil smiled and Zach realized he sounded like a child on a journey asking his parents, "Are we there yet?"

"Be patient my young friend," the scientist replied

as he painstakingly slotted the last circuit board into the device. "I must get this right the first time. A malfunction could cost a life."

Nick raised his eyebrows. "Take your time, doc."

"Yeah, but hurry," Logan urged.

Dr. Jefferson smiled as he began piecing the other components together like a complex jigsaw puzzle.

The four boys were sitting in the laboratory on stools against the far wall where they were out of the good doctor's way. Sheriff Hawkins had returned to Icy Creek where he was needed to help coordinate the ongoing search.

"I'm sorry it's taking so long boys, but the first time I did this I had Dirk's help."

"Who's Dirk?" Nick queried.

"Dirk Wyler," Albert answered with a brief glance their way. "He used to be my partner."

"He's that other guy, the one we heard on the disc talking with Austin," Zach reminded Nick.

"Yes, one and the same," Albert confirmed. "He left work the day of the computer crash and hasn't been heard from since."

"The weasel knew Rylan Jackson was onto him and made his break for it," Logan surmised.

The room fell quiet. The only sounds were those made by Dr. Jefferson as he diligently reassembled the machine.

Time wore on and the afternoon came. Roughly around three Albert stood back to admire his work. It was complete. In haste, he loaded the boys and the machine into the black government pickup and took a turn down a dirt track the boys had not noticed before, behind the facility. They drove for at least half an hour before stopping in the center of the unused road.

"Here seems like an inconspicuous spot to set up our gear." Albert climbed from the vehicle.

"Our gear?" Logan questioned.

The older man grinned. "My gear." He removed the tarpaulin from the back of the truck. There sat the hawk in its case, surrounded by other metal boxes of various sizes.

The boys watched the scientist drag it out and then set up a myriad of scientific gadgets and finally a laptop computer. Zach was almost drooling over the expensive equipment.

"Cool." His eyes gleamed brightly. He looked like he had died and gone to heaven.

Logan just shook his head and smiled. He would obviously prefer a fishing rod and reel any day. Another ten minutes and Dr. Jefferson was ready to start the search.

"So, how's this going to work?" Nick asked.

Wil silently watched the proceedings, totally overwhelmed by the complexity of the scientist's tools.

"H5-40 has an inbuilt map of this entire mountain range. As it travels over the terrain it adds details to its internal memory." Albert removed the hawk from its case with Nick's help.

"So it's a smart machine?" Zach summarized.

"Yes, exactly. I will control the search by giving it a map grid to start in. It will then systematically cover every section of each grid I ask it to. Its search will be thorough and complete."

Wil smiled with understanding. "Plus it can get into places we can't."

"Yes." Albert's attention focused on the device he was positioning on the grass by the side of the track.

"And it's fast," Nick remarked.

Zach remembered the speed at which it had flown through the woods toward them only last week.

"Faster than a racing car." Albert's eyes sparkled with pride in his invention.

Logan leaned against the tray of the pickup. "Okay, let's get it goin' before it gets dark."

"Darkness won't affect this marvel of human ingenuity." Albert used his laptop to power up the device. It lifted into the air, its internal motor making a whirring noise. "It relies on, among other things, heat sensors to track living targets."

Zach had a sudden concern. "It won't gas Laina if it

finds her will it?"

"No. I've altered its setting so that it is on 'seek'."

"Yeah, but didn't you say to Austin that it was on 'seek' when it gassed the guys?" Wil countered, apparently remembering that awful day.

Dr. Jefferson smiled reassuringly. "I've tweaked it since then. It has several other settings now; 'seek', 'seek and neutralize', or 'seek and destroy'."

Logan blew out his cheeks. "Let's just hope it works."

"Please God, let it work?" Zach breathed, his eyes fixed on the newly reconstructed device hovering over the edge of the road.

"Yeah, God," Logan added his agreement, "what he said."

Albert frowned in concentration and tapped away at the keys on his laptop. Suddenly the shiny black machine tilted and shot into the trees, disappearing from sight.

"Let the search begin," Wil commented under his breath as he listened to the whirring engine fade into the distance.

18

Laina's head tossed back and forth as dreams and reality melded into one enormous feverish nightmare. Her eyes opened wide like saucers just as a bear was sinking its ferocious teeth into her right leg. She gasped and sprang upright. Darkness had fallen and so had an eerie silence. Mercifully there was no bear. It was just a dream. However, the pain in her leg was very real. She felt so hot and thirsty. Water. She needed water.

Laina dragged herself the few feet to the creek. She cupped water in her hand and lifted it to her dry lips. She did this several times until her thirst abated and then splashed her face and neck to cool down. Her head felt like it was swimming. Fever. It had to be the infection.

She dampened her t-shirt and then sank to the ground beside the creek in exhaustion. She was so tired. Stars glittered overhead, just barely visible through the narrow gap in the foliage above the creek. They seemed to dance and swirl together in a graceful waltz. Something in the back of Laina's hazy thoughts told her this was not normal. She fought to keep her eyes open but lost the battle only minutes later.

~

"Found anything, doc?" Wil asked in a soft voice.

He had come to stand beside Dr. Jefferson, who was sitting in the tray of the truck. The older gentleman was staring wearily at his laptop screen tracking the movements of the hawk. It was scanning terrain, one map grid at a time, feeding back data and visual information. Meanwhile the boys were stretched out inside the vehicle fast asleep. It was well past midnight and they were still unsuccessful.

"You know," Albert replied thoughtfully as disappointment dampened his initial enthusiasm, "they may not even be in the mountains. For all we know, Austin may have taken Rylan and Laina in the helicopter. They could be anywhere by now." He sighed wearily.

It was a massive area to comb. Yet with the hawk, they had covered more ground in thirteen hours than the search parties had in four days. Wil fought back dejected tears. He had been so sure this would work.

Suddenly Albert's computer started making beeping noises and the screen flashed with images H5-40 was transmitting. A red blip on the map grid beside the video projections blinked in one spot, indicating that the machine had stopped over one particular location. The image displayed on the screen was infrared, yet the orange and red shape in the midst of blackness was distinctly human.

"We've got something!" Albert shouted over his shoulder to the sleeping boys.

They roused quickly, blinking sleepily and crowding around Albert's computer.

"What is it?" Zach asked in a gravelly voice.

"It's a person, that's what!" Logan leapt and whooped for joy.

The boys broke into jubilant celebration while Albert snatched up his cell phone and quickly punched in 911. He would make an anonymous call, give the authorities the location coordinates, and then monitor the person on his screen using the hawk. The second Search and Rescue arrived, he would withdraw the machine, keeping its role in this remarkable find a delightful secret.

~

Laina was just about to bite into a large juicy pizza with melted cheese oozing from its sides. She opened her mouth wide, the tantalizing aroma filling her senses. Her stomach rumbled. No, it pounded. Wait, that couldn't be her stomach. The strange thumping sound intruded upon her dream, growing incessantly louder.

She opened heavy eyelids, and still lying on her back, stared up through the trees into the night sky. It seemed to be ablaze. Shafts of light penetrated thick foliage that swayed violently with a strong wind. The pounding and thwacking continued, a nasty interruption to the serene landscape.

Lights passed overhead and Laina's cloudy mind realized it was a helicopter. Her immediate instinct was to run. Well, no chance of that. Fear gripped her. Had Austin come back?

Who cares who it is! Better to die quickly by one of Austin's bullets than to suffer a slow death by starvation and infection. What if it's a rescue team? Please God, let it be help?

The helicopter seemed to hover nearby, however Laina could not see where it was through all of the trees. She tried to sit up and failed. Her body was weighted by fatigue. She simply had no strength left. The helicopter withdrew and then she was able to hear twigs snapping over the rise to her right.

No, don't leave!

"Is anyone out there?" a male voice shouted from

close by.

Laina closed her eyes in relief and tears slipped from beneath her eyelids, trickling down the sides of her face. She took a deep breath and mustered the strength to call back.

"I'm over here!"

"Laina Jackson?"

As his footsteps crunched over the rise, a familiar whirring sound disappeared into the night.

"You're late," she informed the stranger dryly.

A beam of light from a torch passed over the creek bed and then flashed back to the ragged form sprawled amongst dried leaves. "How's that?"

Laina smiled. "I put in a request heavenward four days ago to be rescued." Her voice was croaky from lack of use.

There was a low chuckle as footsteps splashed through the creek. The sound of static accompanied his approach as he presumably spoke into a hand held radio. "I've found her. Give me five minutes and I'll fire a flare up through the trees so you'll know where to lower the harness."

A pair of boots finally appeared near Laina's shoulder. The stranger crouched to her level and she saw that the torch was built into his helmet. Although it was bright, she was able to look up into a stubbly, smiling face.

"Yeah well, I'm sorry about that. You were a little difficult to find." He hooked the radio onto his belt.

"I don't suppose you happened to bring a pizza with you?"

That comforting chuckle came again, wrapping itself around her like a warm blanket. "Sorry little lady, there's no pizza."

"It's a shame." Laina fought drooping eyelids. "I dreamt I was just about to bite into a very large slice dripping with cheese. Then your helicopter woke me up."

"Well then, I'd better make it up to you. How about we get you out of here and then you can have a real meal?" He removed a first aid pack from his back and began unzipping compartments.

"Sounds like a dream come true." Laina smiled and silently thanked God.

"I'm Nate by the way." His hands gently ran along her shoulders, arms and then her legs to check for injuries and bleeding.

Laina gasped when his fingers found the indentation in her right shin.

"Wow, you've done a pretty good job of breaking this leg," he remarked and began fishing through his pack for an inflatable splint. "And it's infected. Are you hurting anywhere else? How does your back and neck feel?"

"Okay. I think my left ankle is sprained." Laina gritted her teeth as Nate carefully removed her shoes.

"Yup, you've done a good job of that one too. It's swollen. Tell me, what did you do to yourself?"

"I fell out of a helicopter."

"Very funny." He chuckled.

"I wasn't kidding." Laina's teeth suddenly began to chatter. She had been hot only moments ago and now all she could feel was the chill seeping into her body from the cold ground.

Nate marveled. "Then you've got nine lives, minus one. In a little while I'll get you to tell me all about it. For now let's get you ready to travel. The chopper will be back any minute."

"Pizza, here we come."

Nate laughed softly causing Laina to smile. Relief washed over her in waves and she released the struggle to survive into Nate's capable hands.

~

"Have they got her?" Zach asked the scientist who was still peering at his computer screen from the back of the pickup truck.

It was only an hour away from dawn and the four boys were still crowded around Dr. Jefferson, straining to see the visuals provided by H5-40.

"Yes. I've recalled the hawk."

"How long till it gets here?" This question came from Nick.

"Yeah, we wanna get to the hospital," Logan inserted. "That's where the rescue chopper will take her, won't it?"

"Of course that's where it's going," Zach replied logically. "Let's go, doc."

"Now hang on a minute boys." Albert sat his laptop aside. "It'll take H5-40 at least half an hour to get back."

"But I thought you said that thing was fast!" Wil was surprised and also looking a little impatient.

"It is. It's also a very long way away. Now, let's pack up all of this equipment while we wait." Albert's voice was uncharacteristically tinged by irritation, born of an extremely long and stressful past five days.

Nick sighed, reluctantly seeing the older man's point. The other three looked like they were ready to either hijack the vehicle or sprint back to the laboratory on foot.

"Come on, guys," he encouraged. "Dr. Jefferson's done a lot for us. It won't hurt to help him pack up. Besides, the time will go more quickly if we're doing something."

"I guess you're right," Wil conceded.

Albert nodded in satisfaction and the five of them set to work.

~

"Caroline?" Desa called.

Caroline stopped and turned to see her colleague jogging to catch up with her. Her short dark hair bounced as she approached. They were in one of the many long corridors throughout the large three story hospital in Walkerville.

"What's the matter?" She was slightly worried. It was not like her colleague to run, nor was it common that an anxious frown appear on her usually smiling face.

Desa stopped in front of her and took a moment to catch her breath. Caroline waited with mounting curiosity. Finally the woman was able to speak.

"The girl that went missing, the one you said is friends with your son..."

Caroline was instantly alert. "Yes?"

"They've found her!"

"How do you know this?"

"A helicopter just landed on the helipad and the girl was wheeled into the ER."

Caroline had just been headed for a coffee. Having only an hour until her night shift ended, she needed the caffeine. Now she spun and hastened toward Emergency. Desa's voice called after her. Caroline could hear her friend but she did not stop to listen.

She jogged down familiar corridors, passing nurse stations, until she finally reached the emergency room. She scooted past the main desk and then triage. She passed several gurneys separated by curtains, most of which were occupied, until she reached one down the end of the rectangular room where a doctor was just entering. Caroline slipped in behind him just as two nurses brushed by on their way out.

"Laina, isn't it?" the doctor spoke in a calm, friendly tone.

"Mmm," the drugged patient replied, forcing her sleepy eyes open.

"The paramedic was just telling me your story." He began examining her broken leg. "It's quite an amazing tale."

Caroline was used to seeing grisly injuries. However, she was not prepared for the emotions that assailed her when her anxious gaze rested upon her son's best friend.

Laina was in a fresh hospital gown, yet she looked anything but clean. There were scratches and cuts from her head to her feet that were caked with dried blood. Her left ankle was brown and yellow from bruising. Her right leg was swollen, weeping and distorted.

Strangely that was not what struck Caroline the most. The knife that sliced through her, was the realization that this could be her son lying there. They were the same age. If that was Zach, Caroline would be out of her mind with distress. Laina had no one.

Something happened in Caroline's heart at that moment. She could not define the emotion that stole over her, yet she instinctively knew that it changed everything. Nothing was going to make her leave that girl's side short of death or natural disaster!

19

The boys burst through the entrance to Walkerville Hospital, going straight to the front desk where a receptionist was talking on a telephone. Dr. Jefferson had kindly dropped them off before heading home to get some sleep.

Zach and Logan leaned on the front counter, their fretful eyes boring into the middle-aged African American woman on the phone. Nick and Wil flanked them, Nick impatiently tapping out a rhythm with his fingers on the counter. Wil ran a restless hand through his hair, thinking that if he had to wait one more moment he would lose his mind.

At last the receptionist rested the telephone in its cradle and glanced up at the four teenagers standing over her. "Can I help you?"

"We're looking for Laina Jackson. A rescue chopper should have brought her in over an hour or so ago," Zach spoke on behalf of the group.

"The girl that's been on the local news?"

"Yeah, that's the one," Logan confirmed.

"Zach?" a familiar feminine voice spoke from behind them.

"Mom?" Zach spun around. They must have walked straight past her in the waiting room on their way in.

"I'll take it from here," Caroline offered kindly to the receptionist who smiled in return.

The four boys gave Zach's mother their full attention and she hurried to reassure them.

"Laina's okay."

"Where is she?" Nick asked.

"She's in surgery." Caroline saw the alarmed expressions on each of the four faces and held up a hand to stem the barrage of questions that were about to fly at her. "She has a badly broken leg which is unfortunately infected."

Zach frowned in puzzlement. "Isn't it risky to operate when there's infection?"

Caroline was not surprised that he knew this. Living in the same house as a nurse meant the occasional story from work made its way home. "Yes, it is." She did not try to lighten the gravity of the situation.

"Then why are they doing it?" Nick again beat them to the punch.

"The break is pretty bad and the bone has been out of place for too long. It's affecting circulation. They're worried there might be even more complications if they wait." Caroline's compassionate heart squeezed with the disillusionment and distress she saw in the teenagers' faces. She wondered how their new faith in Jesus would survive under the pressure of yet another trial.

~

"Where's Dad?" Laina asked groggily hours later.

She had been transferred to a ward after her surgery and had been in and out of consciousness. Yet this was the first time she had spoken coherently.

Caroline, who was sitting in a chair beside the bed, leaned forward and rested her elbows on the mattress.

"They haven't found your uncle Rylan yet."

"No, I want Dad," she asked more strongly, looking around in disorientation.

Caroline gently took her bandaged hand in her own. "Your dad's in heaven, remember?"

Yes, that was right. The past came flooding back, crashing over Laina like a tidal wave. The smell of the sterile environment triggered a distant memory.

"Dad?" Laina wondered why her head was pounding and puzzled over why every part of her body ached. She gingerly opened her eyes. Even that hurt. She felt like someone had taken to her with a base-

ball bat. Where was she? And where was her dad?

She peeked out from between swollen and bruised eyelids at what appeared to be a hospital room. A curtain afforded her some privacy from other pa-tients in the ward around her, although presently they were drawn back. Stark white walls reflected light from large windows to her right. A television dangled from a fitting on the roof at the foot of her bed. To her left was a bedside table, a food tray on wheels and an intravenous drip attached to her by a tube.

"Elaina?"

Laina rolled her head on the pillow toward the foreign voice. The man's face was familiar. He looked just like her father. Locks of blond hair fell over a brow creased with worry. The blue depths of his eyes were clouded by grief.

"Uncle Rylan?" Laina blinked slowly. She had only ever seen him in photographs. What was he doing here?

Snatches of memory flitted through her mind. A horn blaring, a truck bearing down on her, her fa-ther's panicked face, spinning... then nothing. Had something happened to him? Was that why Rylan was here?

Dread began to mount. "Where's Dad?"

"He's dead," Rylan seemed to push the words past

a constriction in his throat.

"No, I was just talking to him in the car."

Rylan said nothing, which was worse than if he had tried to argue. It was real.

"Laina?" Caroline's anxious voice finally broke through the images of the past that were surfacing.

Laina could not stop the tears that began to flow. She could no longer repress the memories. She covered her face with two bandaged hands and let them fall, her body shaking with silent sobs.

"Laina."

She could not answer. The grief resting heavily upon her chest was too great.

Just then the boys re-entered. If the few food stains on their clothing could be trusted, they must have slipped out to grab a bite to eat in the hospital cafeteria. Laina drew every fiber of strength she had left, to summon control of her emotions upon their arrival. She wiped the trails of moisture from her cheeks and assessed the gathering.

Logan opened his mouth to speak and then quickly closed it. He froze in the doorway, while Nick quietly went to the foot of the bed. Wil sat in the chair opposite Caroline on the other side and waited in awkward silence. Zach's vision blurred with unshed tears. He went to his mother's side and simply stood there, looking rather helpless.

Jay.H.Dee

"Is he dead too?" Laina's voice sounded frighteningly detached, even to her own ears. She blinked wearily.

"Who?" Caroline asked gently.

She turned to the older woman to answer. "Uncle Rylan."

"No, honey, I told you, they haven't found him yet."

"There were gunshots..." She suddenly clammed up, for some inexplicable reason unable to speak of what she had seen and heard.

She had told Nate everything in the helicopter. Why couldn't she make the words leave her lips now? Could one of those shots have killed her uncle? She squeezed her eyes shut tightly, trying to block out the memories.

"What gunshots, Laina?" Logan moved further into the room, coming to stand beside Nick.

That scent... disinfectant. The memories it evoked taunted her and suddenly she wanted out of this place. It hurt too much to be reminded of all she had lost.

"What gunshots?" Logan persisted, his brows drawn together in concern.

"Was it Rylan?" Nick interjected.

Laina tossed back the thin blanket covering her and tried to sit up. She attempted swinging her legs over the edge of the bed, managing to move her right only an inch before pain spiraled through it. And what was that cord attached to her? She was just reaching to rip out the IV needle when two pairs of hands restrained her. Zach grabbed her wrists while Caroline pushed her against the pillows with strong hands on her shoulders.

"What are you doing?" Zach did not have to fight hard to hold her down, even though she struggled against him.

"Laina, stop it!" Caroline commanded.

Logan, Wil and Nick watched on in astonishment.

"I want to go home," she gritted out between clenched teeth and fought against the hands pressing her to the mattress. "Let me up!"

"You can't go anywhere," Caroline explained. "You're too dehydrated and you've got a nasty infection."

"Get me out of here!" They had to let her go. They just had to!

"Call a nurse." Caroline glanced at Wil as she issued this order.

Wil shot out of his seat and dashed from the room, clearly upset and somewhat panicked. Some part of Laina's rational mind told her to calm down. She was scaring everyone. However, her desperation was greater.

"Calm down," Zach entreated, tears in his eyes.

"What is this about?" Caroline almost shouted into her face.

Completely drained and unable to struggle any longer, Laina lay still, breathing hard. Zach let her go and Caroline pulled the blanket over her again.

"I don't want to stay here," she muttered, eyes pleading with her friends for an escape.

"Why?" Logan asked in confusion, not the only one in the room desperately trying to understand.

"He's gone. They're all gone," she whispered, feeling exhaustion pulling her under. "I hate this place." Her eyes closed and sleep came rushing in, despite her efforts to ward it off.

~

A nurse hurried into the room ahead of Wil and came to the bedside. "What's going on?"

"She tried to get out of bed and we had to restrain her," Caroline answered, automatically checking the IV in the girl's hand. It had survived the struggle thanks to Zach's quick intervention.

"I've never seen her that upset," Nick commented, his anxious heart in his eyes.

"Me either," Logan admitted.

"What do you think it was that distressed her?" The nurse tucked in the sheets that had been pulled loose with the patient's thrashing.

Zach remembered the information Laina had volunteered about her past and made a few deductions. "She lost her dad in a car accident three years ago. She told me she was sitting right beside him when it happened. I hadn't thought about it till now, but I'm guessing she spent time in hospital."

"Do you remember what she just said?" Nick prompted.

"Yeah, something like 'they're all gone'," Logan recalled, also trying to put two and two together.

Caroline sighed. Zach clenched his jaw and fought back a barrage of emotion. Now Laina had lost not only her father but her uncle. He was her only living relative. They may not have had an ideal relationship, but he was still her flesh and blood. "She has no one."

The room was quiet.

"That's not true," Logan broke the smothering silence that had fallen. A steely light entered his green eyes. "And I know how to show her."

Zach frowned in puzzlement. "How?"

Logan's smile gave hint of a concocted plan. "Come with me." He turned and walked purposefully from the room.

Nick, Wil and Zach followed him curiously. Zach wondered what scheme he had come up with this time.

20

CIA agent Brady Fitzgerald frowned as he studied the satellite image his colleague had just handed to him. "When was this taken?"

"Today." Ross Findlay handed him another print-out, this one a map of the Tanner Ranges that stretched for hundreds of miles behind the tiny township of Icy Creek. "He must have gotten desperate because he used a cell phone. It belongs to the pilot. He wasn't on for long, but we were able to triangulate his position to within this grid range. And if you look closely at the satellite photo, you'll see a rather suspicious mound at the edge of this clearing near the base of Mount Agnes."

"It looks to me like a helicopter covered by camouflage netting," Brady observed.

"It's rather rocky terrain on that mountain. I gave the location to the park ranger and showed him this picture. He informed me that in the side of Mount Agnes is a cave."

"Nice place for a hideout, wouldn't you say?" Brady smiled like the cat that had finally caught the canary. They had Keffler.

Ross grinned in return. "Shall we send in a team?"

Brady hesitated, his expression contemplative. "No. Keffler may be there to make the deal. We need to know who is buying the software from him. Continue to monitor all movement in that area."

"Yes sir." Ross turned to go, however Brady's voice stopped him.

"Ross, get a hold of Eric at Astro Enterprises for me. I think he may be able to help us capture Keffler without any bloodshed."

Ross frowned in puzzlement yet moved to obey.

~

"What is this?" Caroline stood and watched with astonished wide eyes as the boys entered Laina's room carrying bundles of flowers, cards and candles.

"This is how many people care about Laina," Nick answered for the group as they wordlessly left to bring in more.

They brought armful after armful, depositing them on every available surface; shelves, the bedside table, the food cart, the window sill and the floor against the walls. Laina stared about in puzzlement at the vast array of color saturating the room.

Caroline's fingers covered her lips and tears glistened in her eyes. She looked about at their surroundings in amazement. Laina frowned in confusion. What was going on?

Logan re-entered, followed by Nick, Wil and Zach with the final load. Laina watched her friends, feeling perplexed. They gathered around her bed after completing their mission.

"Where did all of this come from?"

"Your uncle's front yard," Nick replied with a mischievous smile.

"I don't understand."

"People have been leaving this stuff at your uncle's place over the last few days," Wil explained.

"Why?" Laina was still baffled.

"They did it for you." Logan's usually guarded expression softened. "To show you how much they care."

"Yeah," Zach chimed in. "The whole town loves you."

"This is all for me?" Her eyes widened and she glanced again at the gifts squeezed into every crevice.

Caroline smiled warmly. "I think what these sweet guys are trying to show you, Laina, is that you're not alone this time."

"What exactly are you talking about?" Wariness

crept into her tone. The pain from her past was not something she wished to discuss right now. It was suddenly so fresh and her heart felt exposed and raw.

"When you came to Icy Creek, you had no one," Logan explained.

"But now you've got a family. You've got us," Wil chipped in, his shy eyes gentle with kindness.

"And a whole town," Zach added with a grin.

Laina was unsure how she felt about the whole town knowing her plight. Pity was the last thing she wanted. Yet as she beheld the amazing display of love from an entire community, she shoved those self-centered concerns aside. The reality that people truly cared brought a measure of comfort, and she could not hold back the tears that began to fall.

"Oh no," Nick grumbled. "Now you've gone and done it!"

Logan's hands and shoulders lifted in question. "What?"

"We listened to you and now we've made it worse." Nick looked helplessly at Laina who wiped her cheeks with a bandaged hand and actually laughed. He frowned in bewilderment, which Zach found highly amusing.

"Would someone explain to me what's going on?" Nick's classic expression made it clear he found her confusing.

Laina, Caroline, Zach and Logan broke into chuckles at Nick's expense.

"She's crying because she's happy, doofus," Wil informed him dryly.

"Thanks guys," Laina finally spoke. "It means a lot to me. You mean a lot to me."

"Me?" Nick pointed to himself and frowned.

"No... yes. I mean all of you."

The group laughed as Nick received a playful smack to the back of his head. He gave Logan a shove in return.

"Hey, what's that smell?" Zach sniffed the tantalizing aroma drifting through the doorway.

"Smells like pizza." Wil also drew in a deep breath.

Logan's stomach rumbled loudly. Nick was just about to rib him about it when a gentleman roughly in his thirties, in jeans and a checkered shirt, breezed through the open doorway. He was wearing a backpack. His green eyes scanned the room and the visitors surrounding the bed, then they focused upon Laina.

"Ah," he exclaimed with a mischievous sparkle in his smiling eyes, "just the girl I was coming to see!"

Laina frowned and then beamed at her rescuer. "Nate! I almost didn't recognize you without the stubble."

Nate stroked his chin and grinned. "Had a shave.

Even combed my hair. Wanted to look good for the pretty little lady I met this morning."

Laina looked anything but pretty with all of the cuts and bruises covering her from head to toe, and she knew it. For that reason, she delighted in his kindness and smiled broadly. She introduced him to her friends.

"Is that pizza I can smell?" Zach inquired after introductions had been made. His mouth was beginning to water.

"Sh," Nate hissed and held a finger to his lips. "I had to sneak it past the nurses' station." He removed his backpack and sat it on the foot of Laina's bed. He unzipped it and carefully removed two cardboard boxes. He opened them to exclamations and pleadings from the boys who wanted to share the juicy pizzas inside. "Hold it guys." He held up his hands for quiet. "Ladies first." Nate extended a box toward Laina and grinned.

She laughed and took a piece. He then moved on to Caroline who accepted some also. Minutes later the group was enjoying a feast.

"Hey Laina," Zach spoke around a mouthful of ham, pineapple and drippy cheese.

"Yeah?"

"You're getting it all over your bandages."

Laina held up a hand for inspection. He was right.

"You'll have to hide the evidence when you're done." Nate's eyes gleamed wickedly.

"I can sneak those dirty bandages into someone else's bin if you'd like," Nick offered with a grin.

Caroline took another delicious bite. "Sounds like a plan to me."

"Wow Mrs. D," Logan teased Zach's mother, "you're a real rebel."

She winked. "I try to be."

very long time for this particular innovation.

21

"So what do you say, Eric? Shall we put H5-40 to the test?" Brady Fitzgerald coaxed over the phone.

The head of Astro Enterprises leaned back in his desk chair with a thoughtful expression. Having been briefed by Albert Jefferson on the excellent performance of the machine, Eric was feeling that it was finally time to introduce the hawk to the CIA. Any further adjustments to be made would become evident during its frequent use in real life scenarios like this one.

"Alright. It's yours, for a price of course."

He knew they had been waiting a very long time for this particular innovation. It would hopefully keep a lot of men out of the firing line.

"Deal. We'll come today to collect it and you can talk details with the director."

"You will need to select a group who will specialize in its use. We'll have a training program drawn up over the next few weeks."

"You'll loan us a technician to operate it over the

next couple of days?"

"Can do." Eric nodded decisively.

"Good. We'll be out there directly."

"See you soon, Brady."

The two men hung up simultaneously, each moving into action. They had quite a lot to organize and only a short time in which to do it.

~

Laina felt unbelievably hot and attributed it to the fact that it was summer. The gentle sound of rustling clothes and soft footsteps sank into her awareness and she opened drowsy eyelids.

Standing in the doorway was a fashionably dressed teenager. The girl wore a denim miniskirt and a flattering sleeveless shirt. Her once long dark hair was dyed blond and layered to her shoulders. However, her brown eyes were the same as they had always been, although now they were accentuated by make-up.

Allie Staten's nervous gaze flitted about the hospital room momentarily before resting upon Laina, where her eyes widened in horror.

Laina blinked again, not quite believing that her old friend was standing there. "Allie?"

"Hi." She shifted her weight from one foot to the

other. It was clear she was at a loss for words.

Laina knew she looked awful and that it must be a shock to be confronted with the truth of the news reports.

Guilt chased across Allie's features and she broke the silence. "How are you feeling?"

"I'm alright." It wasn't exactly accurate, but Laina understood that what Allie really wanted was reassurance.

Caroline had stayed for most of the night and Gracie had been in and sat with her that morning. The boys had dropped by after lunch, at which time Laina had forced herself to explain to them in detail what had happened.

Then there had been the visitors she had not expected, such as the police who wanted a statement, and later some reporters with their nosey camera crews. Thankfully the hospital staff had shooed them away before they could wheedle information or get any pictures. And now of all people, Allie had come. All Laina wanted to do was sleep.

"So..." Allie's gaze drifted as she cast about for something to say. "They haven't found your uncle yet."

"No." She could not help wondering what this visit was really about and she was running rather low on trust.

The trendy teenager sidled to the edge of the bed where she studied Laina's leg sticking out from a thin bed sheet, firmly strapped into a splint. Laina decided to be blunt.

"Why are you here?" She calmly held the other girl's guilt-ridden gaze.

Looking even more uncomfortable than before, Allie quietly worked up the courage to say what was burdening her in the awkward minutes that followed.

"I came to tell you I'm sorry. I've treated you badly over the last year."

"Why?" Laina thought she had a pretty good idea, yet knew that Allie needed to fully face the seriousness of her actions.

"I guess I was jealous. You've always been more popular with the guys and I wanted them to like me." She shrugged and dropped her ashamed gaze.

"So you spread the fact my uncle hit me around the school in such a way that it made me look like I was lying to get attention."

Allie's eyes filled with unshed tears. "Yes."

"Did you think I was lying when I told you?" Laina felt old anger surface.

Allie looked at her, tears spilling over her lashes. "Yes. I know now you were telling the truth, but at the time I couldn't stand that you were manipulating people to get what you wanted."

Laina shook her head and shifted her angry stare to the ceiling.

"I'm really sorry." That Allie was desperate for forgiveness was evident in her quivering voice.

There was silence for a full minute. When it did not seem that mercy would be forthcoming, Allie rose to leave. Laina sighed deeply, her anger draining away.

"Yeah, we're both idiots. You for what you did and me for secret pride."

Allie's brows drew together in bewilderment. "What are you talking about?"

"Sure what you did was wrong and it totally hurt. But if I think for one second that I'm better than you because you did the wrong thing, then I'm being prideful and that's just as bad." Laina looked her old friend in the eye. "I forgive you. Will you forgive me?"

Allie was still frowning. "Let me get this straight. I'm the one that's hung it on you for the last year and *you're* apologizing?"

Laina broke into an easygoing smile. "I s'pose."

Allie snorted in amusement and sat back in her chair. "You're a nutcase, but sure, I forgive you."

"Good." Laina decided the atmosphere needed a cheerful lift. "Now that we've gotten that cleared up, do you think you could rustle up some chocolate? The food in this place is seriously lacking sugar."

Allie's smile was relaxed for the first time since her

arrival. "Sure. I think there's a vending machine in the cafeteria."

Laina smiled in relief. "You're a lifesaver."

Allie exited on a chuckle and Laina's smiling eyes lingered on the doorway where her friend had just been. What an unexpected surprise to have their rift healed.

Thank You Lord!

Laina closed tired eyes. She would just rest them for a moment. Sleep was swift in coming.

~

Brady Fitzgerald studied the camera images H5-40 was feeding the laptop propped on Dr. Jefferson's knee. The small clearing not twenty miles from Mount Agnes was swarming with CIA agents waiting for the go ahead to move in on their target. Two helicopters were sitting at rest, blades drooping slightly downward as though they were sleepy and taking a nap before the action.

A small tent had been erected to serve as a command center on the edge of the clearing. Inside was a collapsible table with several chairs. It was upon one of these that Dr. Jefferson was perched, watching the progress of his invention as it closed in upon the villains hiding out in the cave in the mountainside.

The images on the computer screen flashed by in a continuous blur, the hawk clearly travelling at a frightening velocity. Brady had to avert his eyes or become nauseous.

"Is it nearly there?" He chanced another glance at the screen and quickly looked away again.

"Almost." Albert's face was a study in concentration. "When it gets there what do you want me to command it? Seek and neutralize or stand by?"

Brady, who was standing behind the scientist and looking over his shoulder, walked slowly to the tent opening and glanced out at his men who were raring to go. "Tell it to stand by. We don't want to rush this thing. If we're patient, we may be able to kill two birds with one stone."

"Are you expecting Austin to have visitors?" Albert took his eyes off the screen to study the CIA agent curiously.

"Yes. Keffler made a call. Not only did that enable us to triangulate his location, it also allowed us to trace the call to an Iranian businessman, Afshin Farahani." Brady glanced over his shoulder to answer, his arms crossed and his expression pensive.

"And that's who you think he's selling the blueprints to?" Albert's gaze went back to his laptop.

"Yes."

"Then I hope you catch them both."

Brady returned his thoughtful stare to the clearing buzzing with activity. "Me too."

~

"Tell me who you sent the designs to!" Austin Keffler demanded, his fiery gaze burning into Rylan's exhausted eyes.

The captive's hands and feet had been bound with duct tape and he was leaning against a stalagmite several paces inside the cave. Dried blood matted the hair over his right ear where a bullet had grazed past in their heated struggle in the helicopter a week ago.

It felt like a month to Rylan who had been starved, beaten and tortured in that time. He wondered how much more he could take.

"You'll just have to kill me." His voice was flat. He almost wished the crooked CIA agent would.

On the other hand, if his brother Connor was correct about there being a hell, then Rylan was certain he was going there. With that thought in mind, he clung to life. Connor had said there was a way to get right with God but Rylan had rejected it. Only the weak needed God.

Austin smiled sadistically. "Oh, I will. But it's up to you whether it will be quick and painless or slow and deliberate." He grabbed a fistful of his captive's hair.

"Now, who has them?"

Rylan thought of the boys. Because of his selfishness, Laina was dead. He would not allow that same selfishness to destroy them as well. Steel entered his icy blue eyes. "Just get it over with."

Austin's gaze snapped with frustration. He slammed Rylan's head against the stalagmite behind him before releasing his grasp. Rylan slumped to the ground, the cave spinning around him and his head pounding painfully.

While lying on his side, cheek pressed into the dirt, he did something he had not done since childhood. He prayed.

God, if You're forgiving like Connor said, then save me? I know I don't deserve it, but please give me a second chance? I know I pushed You away. I guess I figured I'd think about that stuff when I was old and likely to die. Then Dad and Connor died and I pushed You away again because I was angry. I'm really sorry for everything. Jesus, forgive me? I'm Yours if You'll have me.

Something strange happened during that anguished prayer. Exact moments from Rylan's life flashed before his mind's eye. Every sin, every horrible violent thing he had done to his brother and then his niece, every prideful and materialistic thought. With each incident that came to mind, a question burned within his heart.

Are you sorry for this?

It was the first time he could recollect God speaking directly to him. And as every thought, word and deed came to his attention, his answer was a resounding yes. He was awash with shame. Then after the list of offenses was dealt with, people's faces started flashing before his eyes and a phrase whispered through his thoughts.

Do you forgive these their debts against you?

Rylan found this aspect of getting right with God harder to deal with than facing his errors. He had the impression that if his answer was no, then his dealings with God would halt right there. Fearing that reality, Rylan relinquished his bitterness, his hatred, his anger and his hurt.

Yes, Jesus, I forgive them.

Then, like the sun peeking over the horizon after a dark night, Christ's love began to shed its warmth upon Rylan's heart. In a gentle zephyr, peace drifted over his tortured soul, stilling his fears and banishing his doubts.

Forever it had been settled in heaven. Rylan Jackson was no longer his own. His account with God had been cleared, his debt paid by the One who had gone to the cross of Calvary on his behalf.

22

Logan quietly entered Laina's hospital room that evening and was grateful to find it void of visitors. He moved silently across the dimly lit space to the chair beside her bed and sat down. She was fast asleep as he had expected.

He studied her scratched up skin, a reminder of her close brush with death, and found himself thanking God that she was alive. A troubling question shot into his mind like a fiery dart seeking to destroy his faith.

He observed her flushed face and forehead beaded with perspiration. The fever refused to let go and from the quiet whisperings he heard amongst the staff, they were worried too.

Laina's breathing suddenly became erratic and her head tossed to and fro on her pillow. Logan felt a constricting sensation in his chest and drew his chair closer to the bed. Laina's eyes jerked open and her hands came up as though she was protecting herself. Logan took a bandaged hand, drawing it back to the mattress and holding it there gently.

"Sh," he soothed, as he often did for his little sister when she awoke crying in the night. "It was just a dream."

~

Laina's head turned in the direction of her visitor and her suddenly alert gaze met his. Her breathing evened out as she forced herself to calm down. "I was falling again."

"I thought as much," Logan answered, his usually brusque voice soft and soothing.

Laina was struck by his tenderness and studied him with serious eyes. "This is a side to you I've rarely seen."

Logan dropped his gaze bashfully which made her smile. He started to pull his hand away and she gave it a grateful squeeze before letting go.

"I hope you'll let me see it more often?"

This brought his head up again in surprise. He met her kind gaze and broke into a good-natured grin. "Just as long as the guys don't get wind of it."

"Yeah I know, you've got a reputation to protect. We can't have people knowing you're really a nice guy under that surly exterior."

"Zach's right about you, Laina." Logan's smile was cheeky.

242

She decided to play along. "Is that so?"

"Yep. Somewhere along the line you've swallowed a dictionary." He sat back in his chair, very self-satisfied.

Laina could not resist the laughter that bubbled up within her. It started in her chest and worked its way to her lips. The sound was so delightful that Logan found himself chuckling with her. Laina sighed and a smile remained to light her flushed face.

"Hey, do you think you could ask someone to get some air conditioning going? It's stifling in here."

"The air conditioning *is* going. You're the only one that's hot. You've got a bad fever."

"Oh." That explained a lot. Laina maneuvered her splinted leg so that she could roll onto her side. Logan continued the conversation while she got comfortable.

"The nurses keep giving you stuff to take your temperature down. Personally I'd just dunk you in Icy Creek."

Laina was now able to look directly at him without getting a crick in the neck. "I'd let you." Upon closer scrutiny, she noticed he was not smiling as easily as he had been yesterday. "Something's on your mind. What is it?"

Logan did not seem surprised, which served to confirm her suspicion that something was bothering him. He leaned forward, his elbows resting on his knees, his eyes level with hers. Tiredness tugged at Laina's body, however curiosity and concern kept her awake.

"Do you ever wonder why God let this happen to you? I mean, He could have prevented it, but He didn't. He allowed someone to kidnap you and your uncle, you fell from a helicopter, you nearly died of dehydration and now-" Logan suddenly stopped, seeming to reconsider what he had been about to say.

Laina guessed what he was thinking. The fever. There had to be more to it than people were letting on. She wasn't surprised. Neither was she concerned. She was too exhausted and hot to care.

"And now..."

"And now they're all worried the infection has led to something serious."

Logan looked at her tentatively, reluctant to confirm the truth. Laina read his hesitation.

"Do they think they'll have to amputate?" she forced the horrid question from her mouth.

"I don't know. They're not saying anything at the moment but I can see they're worried."

"I know where I'll spend my eternity. Jesus is there and so is my mom and dad. I'll be in good company." She secretly wished she could go now.

As nasty as he had been at times, she mourned the loss of her uncle. Dealing with the aftermath and compounded grief of losing her last living relative had sapped her of the will to push on. The future held so much uncertainty, and at the moment the thought of sifting through the emotional pain was too much. She was tired, so very tired.

Logan's gaze sparked fire. "Don't you talk like that Elaina Jackson!"

His sudden vehemence took her by surprise. Was she being selfish? Probably.

Logan's tone softened and Laina was stunned to see tears glistening in his eyes. "I can't lose you again."

Laina's own blue depths pooled. "Then how about I stick around." She smiled to reassure him, taken aback by the sudden knowledge of how much he really cared.

"I like that plan a whole lot better," he replied gruffly.

Laina could feel exhaustion pulling her under, and realizing she had not yet addressed his question, she forced herself to stay awake a little bit longer.

"You asked me if I wonder why God let this happen. The answer is a very simple one and it's totally foreign."

Logan leaned forward a little, eager for insight.

"It's not about us."

Logan frowned. Seeing his confusion, Laina went on to explain.

"We humans are incredibly self-centered. We think this thing called life is about us, but it's not. The entirety of life on earth is actually the story of a most majestic God, who created it all and holds it in the balance. He is so incredibly beautiful and He stands center stage. He is the main character, and being the awesome God that He is, He ought to be. Our problem is that our sinful nature tells us lies, inflating our egos and making us think we're bigger than we actually are."

"I'm still lost."

"The story called life is all about God. He loves and values us tremendously, but the attention and the glory are ultimately His. That means the main purpose of our lives is to bring Him that glory.

"When we start asking why God let's bad things happen, we've taken our focus off Him and turned it inward. God will use everything that happens in our lives to bring Him honor, the good stuff and the bad. Our heart's desire should be to reflect His beauty and His character in whatever circumstances this messed up world lands us in; not to ditch Him when we don't get our way. When we do that, we've fallen into the trap of thinking that the story is ours."

Jay .H. Dee

The lengthy explanation left Laina completely drained. "Besides," she reasoned with her last ounce of strength, "if I hadn't been taken, then you boys wouldn't have seen your need for Jesus. I wouldn't want to go through it again, but I look at it as a redeemed situation. Somehow people are going to see how glorious He is. At times when reason eludes me, I just remind myself that it's not about me."

~

Logan sat back in his chair, his mind racing to process this new concept. Laina had been right. Her answer did seem totally foreign. On the other hand, it also made perfect sense. He did often think that he was the center of the universe, or at the very least, the center of Icy Creek.

He was just opening his mouth to admit that fact, when he noticed Laina had dropped off to sleep. He wanted to sit and contemplate her unearthly wisdom, yet was aware his mother would be wondering where he was. With one last glance at his friend, he quietly left the room and started the short walk to the bus stop.

As he rode the bus from Walkerville to Icy Creek, he begged God to rid Laina's body of infection, and greater still, to heal the brokenness in her soul.

247

~

The distant sound of rotor blades grew steadily to a dull roar. Austin leapt from his sitting position against a rock wall, where he had been idly drawing on the dirt floor with a stick. He trotted to the cave entrance.

His apprehensive gaze scanned the sky, spotting an unmarked helicopter approaching at a hasty speed. Its windshield was fixed resolutely in the direction of the clearing like two large eyes intently tracking prey. A foreboding chill ran down Austin's spine. He had finally arrived. And Rylan had not yet divulged the whereabouts of the blueprints.

The crooked CIA agent ran a frustrated hand through his black curly hair. It was not supposed to turn out this way. It had all been going so smoothly until Rylan had thwarted his carefully devised plans.

The blueprints would be in his hands. Dirk would make contact with Afshin Farahani and bring him here for the exchange. Then Austin would pin the crime on Rylan Jackson, take some long awaited leave, and he and Dirk would find a quiet beach in the pacific to inhabit for several months. The Iranians would be happy and Austin and his computer nerd partner would be rich. It had seemed so straightforward. But now... Well, things had gone pear shaped.

He contemplated beating a confession out of Rylan again and then reconsidered. There was no point. The prisoner was just barely conscious from the last time he had tried to extract information. The man simply would not talk and there was a strange sort of tranquility about him. It was almost like he welcomed death.

This aggravated Austin no end. His threats were useless on a man with no fear of dying. Normally he would then move to threaten the man's family. However that was no longer an option. The girl had been killed days ago falling out of the helicopter. Austin's taut nerves were slowly fraying around the edges. This situation was fast becoming a quagmire.

The unmarked helicopter set down gently in the clearing, the long dry grass around it flattening with the billowing wind whipped up by the rotor blades. The door opened and out stepped two gentlemen.

The first was of medium height, with lily white skin from years of being indoors. He wore glasses from a couple of decades of eyestrain and had closely cropped brown hair. It was Dirk Wyler.

Austin's nervous gaze flitted to the second man. A Middle Eastern gentleman in a grey suit adjusted his jacket with a shrug and a casual flick of his lapels. His calm gaze scanned the clearing for the man he was to rendezvous with. His shrewd eyes locked with Austin's. The ex-CIA agent sighed and started to walk toward Afshin.

They were within five paces of one another when something darted from the woods to their right. The black, triangular shaped glider was upon them, releasing its sleep-inducing gas before they could utter an astonished cry.

~

Less than twenty miles away, Brady Fitzgerald watched the scene unfold over Albert Jefferson's shoulder on his laptop.

Albert studied the images H5-40 was sending back as it hovered over the unconscious bodies of its targets. "They're down, Mr. Fitzgerald."

"Have it neutralize the pilot and then scan the cave."

"Alright."

Albert fed the device instructions via his laptop and within seconds was viewing footage of the pilot slumped in his seat. Brady watched as it entered the cave and moments later produced images of two more unconscious men inside. One appeared to be the boss's helicopter pilot and the other was Albert's co-worker, Rylan Jackson. From the looks of him, it was anyone's guess whether he was still alive.

"Is that everyone accounted for?"

Albert glanced over his shoulder at the man standing behind him. "Yes. H5-40 isn't picking up any more life readings."

"Good. Time to send the team in." Brady strode to the tent doorway and gathered his agents with a shout.

After a quick explanation and several instructions, the group piled into the helicopters. The large beasts took off, their noses pointing determinedly in the direction of their targets. Meanwhile Albert recalled the device lest it take out the CIA too.

~

Friday morning Caroline strode into Laina's room.

"Good morning. You're looking terribly alert today." She took a seat by the bed.

Another patient occupied the bed closest to the window, having been admitted the night before. The older woman was asleep, for which Caroline looked grateful.

Laina's gaze followed her friend, missing nothing. There was a forced cheerfulness in her demeanor.

"Hi yourself. What day is it?"

"It's Friday. A week to the day you were abducted."

Caroline carefully searched Laina's face.

"Oh." Laina's expression was cautious. Something was definitely up. "I woke up in the middle of the night and it was like the cloud around my brain had lifted and I could think. My head feels so clear today. I think maybe everyone's prayers are being answered."

Caroline touched the back of her hand to Laina's forehead. "I think you're right. Your fever's gone. How does your leg feel?"

Laina shrugged. "It feels fine. There's a bit of a dull ache, but that's all."

This time Caroline's smile was genuine. "Isn't our God good!"

"Yeah, He is." Laina wondered about the hesitance she was reading in the other woman's countenance.

"We've all been very worried about you." Caroline seemed to gauge how to broach what was on her mind. "How are you coping?"

Laina frowned. Where was this heading? "With what?"

"With everything that's happened."

Laina's pensive gaze wandered. The regular hospital sounds drifted in and out of the room, accompanied by background noise provided by the television in its brace in the roof at the foot of the bed. "I haven't allowed myself to think about it much. At the moment I guess I'm just surviving."

Caroline's face gained an expression Laina was not comfortable with. The seriousness in her eyes and the way she paused to tactfully word her thoughts told her that in the next few minutes, her life would once again be flipped upside down.

"What's wrong?" Laina watched as Caroline seemed to struggle with whatever it was she had to say, and felt a sinking feeling in the pit of her stomach. Had they found her uncle? Was he dead?

"There are two things."

Laina waited, shoring up her heart for yet another blow.

Caroline took a deep breath and plunged in. "They've found your uncle Rylan. He's been badly beaten but they think he'll be alright."

Laina sighed with relief. He was alive. "And the guy that did it?"

"He's in custody."

Laina was puzzled. "That was good news, so why do you look like your pet dog just died?"

Caroline could not resist a smile. "There's more."

Laina swallowed hard. "Okay."

"Sheriff Hawkins has been in touch with the welfare department, and I must admit that I have as well."

Laina's eyes lit with understanding. So she was

about to be uprooted again. Well, this time she had choices and she refused to go.

She abruptly threw back the covers and swung her legs over the edge, gritting her teeth against the discomfort that followed. Caroline's eyes widened in astonishment and then Laina saw her brows knit in concern.

"Where are you going?" There was a worried edge to her voice.

"I have a life here in Icy Creek and I am not about to leave it all behind and start again with a bunch of strangers. I've been there before and I'm not going there again!" Laina stood, bearing her weight on her good leg, and reached for the crutches leaning against the wall near her bed.

"Slow down a minute."

Laina's back was momentarily to her and Caroline hastened to explain.

"I've asked the department to grant me guardianship."

Laina froze with one crutch under each arm. She slowly turned around and her astounded gaze met Caroline's. "You what?"

Uncertainty played across Caroline's features. "I said I've asked the department to grant me legal guardianship." She rushed on to give the details, obviously afraid Laina would shut the conversation down and walk out. "They were going to place you with a family from Walkerville but when I explained your situation further and how much I've come to care for you, they said they might consider placing you with us. Of course there are details to be taken care of, red tape and such..."

Laina was astonished. "You want me to live with you?"

Caroline stopped babbling long enough to notice tears pooling in the teenager's eyes. "Yes."

A sob escaped Laina's lips and then another until she was crying uncontrollably. She stood there with tears rolling down her cheeks in rivulets, her face angled downward and her crutches still under her arms.

"Laina, what is it?"

She drew in a deep breath to stem the tide of emotion and met Caroline's helpless gaze across the bed. "I haven't been wanted in a very long time." The simple confession was painful to admit.

Sorrow clouded Caroline's expression. She walked around the bed and drew Laina into her arms, unable to stop her own tears.

At least five minutes had passed before Laina was able to gain control. When she did, she pulled away and smiled. Caroline smiled in return and patted the bed, urging her to sit down. She complied, allowing the older woman to take the crutches from her hands. She wiped her cheeks with a bandaged hand. Having leaned the crutches against the wall, Caroline then sat in her regular chair.

"Do you think the department will go for it?" Laina felt hope bud for the first time since her arrival at the hospital.

"I don't know, but I'm optimistic. The gentleman I talked to is coming to see you today. That's why I needed to break the news now. I didn't want it coming as a shock from a total stranger."

Laina tried to process this information and found that her mind was reeling. "What about Zach? What does he think?"

Caroline smiled. "I mentioned it to him this morning and he said it was about time the rubber hit the road."

"Huh?"

Caroline chuckled. "He meant our faith. It's time we put it into action."

A slow smile crossed Laina's face. Wow! Zach had clearly undergone a huge change in the last few days. "And Uncle Rylan? What if he says no?"

The gleam in Caroline's eyes dimmed and her smile disappeared. "Laina, he doesn't get a say in the matter. Because of his abuse, the department is stepping in and forcefully removing you, whether he likes it or not."

Laina did not know how she felt about this. The incident in the helicopter had shown her that he cared, while at the same time he had problems he needed to deal with if his behavior was to change.

"So what do I do?"

Caroline smiled understandingly. "Kick back and relax. The man won't be in until this afternoon. What were you watching?" she abruptly changed the subject and indicated the television that was still on.

Laina saw through her tactic and was grateful. An ordinary topic would definitely help restore some normalcy to the day.

She shrugged. "Nothing really. I've kind of gotten used to not having a TV. I'd much rather read."

Caroline grinned. "Then do you mind if I watch the breakfast show?"

"Sure, if you pass me that Bible on my bedside table."

Caroline passed her the sacred book and then picked up the TV remote. Laina opened to Psalms, knowing that her favorite Scriptures would help to calm her anxious spirit. She was in between Psalm ninety-one and ninety two when Caroline made her first channel change. Another minute later the older woman flipped stations. Laina's interest peaked when yet again three minutes later, Caroline was surfing.

Laina closed the Bible and glanced sideways at her friend. Caroline met her gaze with an innocent expression.

"What?"

"I've just discovered that you're a channel surfer."

"What's so bad about that?" Caroline challenged as a hint of a smile made an appearance.

"It's annoying."

"Tough luck kid."

Laina chuckled. "I hereby dub thee flip."

"Huh?" Caroline slanted Laina a curious look.

"I'm gonna call you flip from now on."

"Zach's right, honey. You *have* swallowed a dictionary." She winked.

Laina shook her head in mock exasperation and went back to reading. All the while she sensed hope growing within her. Living with this lively woman she had come to love like a mother would be a dream come true.

23

"I want to see Laina," Rylan called groggily for the umpteenth time, trying to gain the nurses' attention.

"Can someone just tell the girl he's asking for her?" the doctor on duty asked testily on his way past the nurses' station. He had been listening to the patient's distressed pleas all day since he had learned that his niece was alive.

There were two staff members at the desk. One was working on a computer and the other leaned on the counter waiting for the information she had requested. The latter rolled her eyes in exasperation.

"We can't. The welfare department is involved."

"Has someone explained that to him?" The doctor stopped in front of the counter, a clipboard in his hands.

"We tried. It only upset him and he demanded to see her all the more," the nurse at the computer replied.

Laina, dressed in clean shorts and a T-shirt with a crutch under each arm, inadvertently listened to the conversation from several paces away.

Caroline had stopped also, having come with Laina to visit her uncle upon her request. Rylan's distraught appeal had stopped Laina in her tracks. She had never heard him so upset before. Then to hear that he had been denied access brought an unexpected wave of displeasure. How could the department be so cruel?

"Are you sure you want to do this?" Caroline quietly asked the teenager beside her.

"Of course." Laina felt a good measure of irritation at the world. He would not hurt her here, and for all the abuses in the past, in his own way he did care about her.

She moved into view of the hospital staff. "I'm Laina Jackson. I want to see Uncle Rylan." Her resolute gaze did not waver.

The trio at the desk glanced her way in surprise. The two nurses looked uncertain, while the man in the long white coat appeared to be relieved.

"He's right this way." The doctor directed Laina and Caroline toward a room close to the nurses' station on their right.

"I don't think it's such a good idea," the nurse at the computer started to object.

"I don't care what welfare says," Laina tossed over her shoulder, "he's my uncle." She followed the doctor into the single room and paused in the doorway while he went straight to the patient's side.

Laina's shocked gaze was riveted upon the man lying in bed, bruised and swollen from head to foot. Both of his arms were plastered, as was his right leg. He was barely recognizable. What had Austin Keffler done?

It occurred to her then that falling out of that helicopter had actually saved her life. Seeing the nasty CIA agent's work for herself, she was certain that had she not fallen, she would be dead right now. The only reason Rylan was alive was because he had held valuable information, and killing him would have ended any chance of retrieving it.

"Mr. Jackson." The doctor looked down into the patient's battered face.

"I want to see my niece."

"She's here."

There was no missing the huge sigh that escaped the injured man's split lips. The doctor beckoned to Laina with a gesture of his hand, and feeling numb all over, she had to force her body to comply. The doctor left when she reached the patient's side. Caroline pulled the chair beside the bed closer and Laina sat down, her eyes glued to her uncle.

"Laina?" Rylan peered out from beneath purple and blue lids.

She felt the numbness slowly leaving. "Yeah, it's me."

Rylan licked dry, cracked lips. When he spoke, his voice was hoarse. "I have to tell you something."

Laina's hands started to tremble and then the rest of her followed suit. She told her body to stop it and be still, but it would not listen. The rational part of her mind said it was shock and that she should calm down. Yet to her dismay, she found that her brain had no control over her physical reaction. Caroline's reassuring hand rested on her shoulder, giving her the courage and presence of mind to respond.

"Okay."

Silent tears trickled from Rylan's eyes down his bruised skin and into his ears and hairline.

"I thought you were dead, and when they told me you were alive, I knew I had another chance to say how sorry I am. I've treated you horribly from the first day you arrived and I think I owe you an explanation."

Laina was staggered. Rylan had never apologized to her for anything. She sat in a stunned stupor while he went on.

"I've been taking my anger with my father out on you."

"What do you mean?" What did her grandfather have to do with this?

"My father was always a difficult man to please. It didn't matter how hard I worked or how much money I earned, he was never happy with me. But he was different with your dad." Rylan studied her as best he could as he poured out his painful past.

Laina's mind started to reel for the second time that day as the last few years finally began to make sense.

"Connor had a wife and then later a daughter our father loved."

Rylan's expression was a mixture of shame and open honesty, both traits that Laina had never witnessed in him.

"I had no children and I wasn't about to marry just to please Dad. I couldn't compete with Connor. He had Dad's undivided affection and approval and I could never match up.

"Connor talked with him about it and even tried to make it up to me, but I wouldn't listen. By that stage I was so jealous I hated them both. So I moved out here and started a life of my own without them. Then when your father died I felt bad about the rift between us, so I took you in." Rylan drew a ragged breath. Clearly his confession was costing him.

"I never really hated you. I was just angry at Connor because he was the favorite and I felt bad that he had died before I could put it right. Unfortunately

I never knew how to manage what I was feeling so you copped the brunt of it. For that I'm sorry." His earnest gaze held hers. "I hope that one day you can forgive me?"

Laina blinked back unshed tears. "Uncle Rylan, I've already forgiven you. Besides, it's not my forgiveness that you really need."

Rylan's split lips stretched into a small smile. "I know. I've put it right with God the way Connor said I had to, and I know He's forgiven me. That's why I'm asking for yours."

Laina's eyes widened with yet another surprise. "You've accepted Jesus?"

"Yes."

An amazed smile lit her face. "Wow! That's incredible!"

"I *am* sorry for everything."

Laina's smile vanished with the shame and deep regret she read in his countenance. "I forgive you, Uncle Rylan."

Rylan sighed with relief, his head turning on the pillow so that he again faced the roof. His relieved eyes closed. Suddenly he opened them and looked at her from beneath black and blue lids. "They said welfare is moving you."

Caroline stepped forward, a hand still upon Laina's shoulder. "We've talked with your niece's caseworker today. It seems Laina is coming to live with my son and I."

"You're from around here?" Rylan's tone had become brusque.

"Yes. We recently moved to Icy Creek and we plan to stay."

He nodded and shifted his limited vision to the roof. "Good. I wish I could take you back and have a second chance," he spoke to Laina with his gaze averted, "but I don't trust myself. My experience with God is real, but it's gonna take awhile before I get some things in my life straightened out."

"I think that's very wise," Caroline stated, renewed respect in her eyes.

Rylan asked for more details, and while he and Caroline talked, Laina sensed an incomprehensible peace settle over her. This felt right. She would live with Caroline and Zach, and Rylan would grow in his new faith and sort out the issues in his life.

She had hope that eventually their relationship would be fully restored. Deep within her spirit, she knew that it was only a matter of time and God's limitless grace.

Epilogue

"Come on Zach! How long can it possibly take to make yourself gorgeous?" Laina called through the bathroom door, leaning on her crutches. It was their first day back at school and at this rate, they were going to be late.

"Guys don't look gorgeous, they look cool," Zach corrected, his voice penetrating the closed portal.

"Whatever. I never knew boys worried that much about their looks!"

"Yeah well, that's our Zach," Caroline commented pragmatically as she strode past Laina into her room.

Laina's face lit up and she maneuvered her crutches so that she could follow. It was always a pleasure to talk with her new foster mother. She stopped in Caroline's doorway.

"I didn't know you'd gotten back from night shift. How was it?"

"Hectic. There's a new patient in ICU with a serious back injury and all night long he kept pressing his buzzer and crying out for more painkillers." Caroline pulled off her shoes and dumped them on the carpet.

She disappeared into her walk-in wardrobe, continuing the conversation while she changed out of her uniform. "I understand that he's in pain, but honestly, sometimes you just have to suck it up and be brave." She re-emerged from the closet in her grumpy cow pajamas. "So this is your first day back at school. Are you nervous?"

Laina considered the question, her expression thoughtful. "Yes and no."

Caroline removed her earrings as she listened.

"Yes because everyone knows about what happened and it's hard to face them, and no because I've got the guys to hang out with now."

Caroline dropped her second earring into the jewelry box on her dressing table and then moved toward Laina. "You have nothing to be ashamed of. Both the abduction and your uncle's mistreatment were not your fault. Besides, other than your leg in that splint, you've healed up nicely and you look like your old self again."

"I know. I just don't want to be treated different from anyone else." Laina shrugged, the nonchalant gesture belying how she truly felt.

Caroline smiled compassionately and draped an arm around her shoulders, giving her a squeeze. "Just be yourself and pretty soon everyone will see that you're still the same friendly person you've always been." She released Laina and strode up the hallway to the bathroom. "Now, let's see what's taking my vain son so long."

Laina smiled in amusement and followed her. Caroline rapped soundly on the door.

"Zach, you're a handsome, hot lookin' thing. The girls will fall all over themselves the second they see you. You don't need all of that hair gel. Come on, get out of there so Laina can brush her teeth."

The door opened and Zach stared at his mother with a long-suffering expression. "Very funny, Mom."

"I wasn't trying to be funny." Caroline's innocent expression could not fool Zach. "You are a stunning catch, just like your father." With that she planted a kiss on his cheek and sauntered happily down the hallway toward the kitchen.

Zach grimaced and wiped his cheek with a sleeve. "Gross Mom!" He met Laina's gaze and looked irritated that her eyes were brimming with laughter. "Don't you start." He brushed past her, also headed for the kitchen.

"I wouldn't dare. You better eat breakfast quick, you handsome thing, because the guys will be here any minute."

Zach groaned and rolled his eyes and Laina

laughed. She entered the bathroom and located her toothbrush and the toothpaste. She could not wipe the smile from her face as she brushed her teeth. Zach complained and pretended to be offended by the affectionate teasing he received on a regular basis by the women in his house, but Laina could tell that secretly he enjoyed the camaraderie just as much as they did.

Satisfied that her hair was combed and her teeth were clean, Laina made her way to the kitchen. Zach was just buttering a piece of toast when there was a knock on the front door. Laina went to answer it, passing the living room on her way.

"Come in," Caroline called from her place on the sofa, her right hand aiming the remote at the television and her thumb madly working as she surfed through the available channels.

Laina reached the door at the same time Caroline called for whoever was on the porch to enter. The door opened and Nick poked his head in. He spotted Laina only a few feet away from him and grinned. He opened the door fully and stood on the threshold.

"Time to go."

Laina smiled in return. "I'm ready."

"Yeah, me too." Zach came from the kitchen, his backpack slung over his shoulder. Laina's pack was in his left hand and a piece of toast was clutched in his right.

"Bye kids." Caroline smiled.

"See ya Mom." Zach surprised his mother by taking a short detour into the living room to drop a kiss on her cheek.

Caroline beamed with pleasure.

"Yeah, see ya flip." Laina trailed him into the living room. She could not quite keep her balance leaning down to plant a kiss on her foster mom's cheek and so Caroline stood and gave her an affectionate squeeze instead.

She walked them to the door. "Have a great day, both of you."

"Will do." Zach quickly helped Laina put her backpack on. He pulled on his shoes and followed Nick onto the porch.

"Now remember," Caroline reminded them, "if you're tired from walking around on crutches all day, just give me a call and I'll pick you both up. I should be awake by then."

"Thanks for the offer, Mrs. D, but we've got it covered," Nick assured her with a grin. He nodded toward the front gate where Logan and Wil were waiting on their bicycles, which had been retrieved from the forest a week ago.

Attached to the back of Wil's bike was what looked like a homemade cart. Inside the cart the boys had bolted the seat from a discarded chair. Laina hopped to the gate using her crutches and looked down at the invention incredulously.

Her face lit with delight. "Wow guys, this is so cool!"

Zach also admired their handiwork. "Yeah, who came up with this?"

"That would be me," Logan answered with a grin.

"Climb on Laina," Wil invited.

"Yeah, we're running late." Nick got onto his bicycle, which had been leaning against the front picket fence.

"I'll get my bike." Zach dashed for the garage while Laina got comfortable on the cart with her crutches across her lap.

"Are you sure I'm not going to be too heavy to pull along?"

Wil turned in his saddle and grinned at her. "If you are, we'll just attach a rope to Logan and he can help."

Laina smiled broadly and chuckled. "This is gonna be fun!"

"You boys be careful with my girl," Caroline warned from the porch where she surveyed the contraption dubiously.

"We will Mrs. D," Nick promised and waved.

He and the guys turned in the driveway and rolled

onto the road. Laina waved at Caroline and returned her beaming smile to the road ahead. Zach caught up and the group pedaled down the street.

"Did you guys hear that Austin Keffler and Dirk Wyler are in prison?" Zach asked his friends.

"Yeah, Dan Fisher told Wil's dad about it yesterday," Nick replied as they rode along at a steady pace.

Logan was curious. "Does anyone know what happened to the creep that was buying the blueprints for the hawk?"

"Dan said he's in the slammer too for trying to buy stolen stuff... or something like that," Nick answered.

"And what about H5-40?" Wil jumped into the conversation.

"H5-40?" Laina queried, feigning ignorance. "What's that?"

The boys glanced at her and broke into chuckles, obviously remembering the promise they had made to Astro Enterprises to keep their inventions and their very existence a secret.

"I don't know," Zach answered with comically wide eyes. "Do you?"

"Not me," Logan answered with a grin.

"Maybe we could find out?" Nick joked with a mischievous expression.

Laina rolled her eyes.

"I've had my fill of excitement for the year," Wil

commented, his remark closely mirroring Laina's thoughts.

"Oh I don't know about that," Zach teased with gleaming eyes. "I could handle another conspiracy."

The group glanced at each other as they rode around the bend and pedaled toward school, each set of eyes sparkling with humor and taking on a hint of mischief.

It was only a matter of time before their sense of adventure got the better of them. Laina smiled contentedly. She had found the place where her heart belonged: in the safe haven of her heavenly Father's arms, and the friendship of an extraordinary group of teenagers.

Dear reader,

I hope you have enjoyed reading this book as much as I have enjoyed writing it. The characters, places and events are purely fictitious and have been a delight to toy with.

The main theme coming through this story for me has been God's centrality. I find that it is so easy to get caught up in the concerns, struggles and issues of life and forget that there is a bigger story unfolding before our eyes.

It is the story of the majestic King of the universe and He is the central character that we all revolve around. We can try to make the story about ourselves and end up living a tiny self-centered life. Yet our glory will fade with our passing.

Or we can position ourselves to be supporting characters that point to the main Character, and allow our lives to reflect His glory. Either way, the bottom line is that whether we live for God or ourselves, He will always get all of the glory.

I have found that putting this principle into action is incredibly liberating. My focus gets taken off me and onto Jesus, and I no longer have to worry about what people think. I need only think of Christ and how I can best reflect Him. Care to take up the challenge and live it for yourself?

Laina reflected this principle and it was how she

came to grips with the tragedies that she had faced in her young life. Zach struggled with the issue of why bad things happen and his anger was misdirected at God. He is representative of many people in the world today who are angry and disenchanted with the suffering all around them. His character is honest and to the point, which I like.

It was fun to put the two characters together and see the way they interacted, and how Laina's strong personal relationship with Jesus Christ impacted Zach and the other boys.

As I write, I wonder where you, the reader, are at in your journey. Are you like Laina, strong in your faith and living for a higher purpose in a bigger plan?

Are you like Zach, struggling with the bad things in life you've faced? Are you fighting God and pushing Him away?

Or are you like Wil and Nick, who have not really thought much about Him, but have a thirsty and receptive heart to receive Him when you are given the opportunity?

Perhaps you feel like Rylan Jackson, laden with shame for the things in your life you feel can never be forgiven?

No matter your point in life, it all boils down to this one question: what are you going to do about what Jesus did for you?

His hand is extended to you in love, beckoning you to come to Him, to tell Him all of your misdeeds and say you're truly sorry. Will you receive His forgiveness and know the amazing reality of His grace?

His grace is able to bring good from even the terrible things that have happened in your life, whether by your doing or from someone else. He wants you to experience His peace, His joy, and His love that has no limits. He wants you to allow yourself to be daily changed more and more into His likeness.

He desires for you to experience His healing, to be set free from past hurts, and to cast off the shackles of fear that bind your soul and keep you from becoming all He wants you to be in Him.

Yes, there will be times of heartache and tragedy, for we live in a world fallen from its former state of perfection. But the difference is that when Jesus is in your life, you no longer have to face those heartaches and tragedies alone. He will strengthen you. He will walk beside you and carry you when you can no longer go on. He will lighten your heart with the music of His love. He will keep you at peace in the midst of life's storms, just as He did for Laina when she faced her biggest trials. Christ's presence is real. He is reality.

I have walked in close relationship with Jesus for many years now and can testify to His faithfulness and His beauty. He colors a dark world, brings hope where there is despair and depression, joy where there is grief, peace where there is turmoil, and beauty where there is the ugliness of sin. Lofty words, I know. But He is well and truly able to live up to them. Try Him and see for yourself if I am right. I dare you!

I know there will be those reading this who already know Jesus personally for themselves. That is awesome! Don't give up, don't give in, don't compromise. The reward will be well and truly worthwhile when we stand face to face with Him in eternity. Press ever closer to His side. Listen to His word and obey it. Surrender all and find that you're actually gaining more than you ever gave up.

Life on this earth is fleeting, with not one minute to lose. Knowing Jesus and loving Him is the reason you're on this planet. Never lose sight of Him or your mission.

And finally, may He be glorified! He is the center, the Star in this story called history. He is the most amazingly beautiful person in the universe, who deserves all praise. I honor You, Lord God Almighty.

To His Daughter

www.jayhdee.weebly.com